The roar grew thunderous...

With a deafening explosion, tons of pipe were expelled up through the rig floor, blasting upward like enormous chunks of shrapnel. The derrick shattered, while from the wellhole, a hissing black column volcanoed heavenward. An oily cloudburst fell in a wide ring about the platform, enveloping the cycloning horse and rider, who immediately disappeared from view.

At a safe distance, the crewmen shouted their alarm, aware of the broken iron and timber flying hidden in the downpour. Nobody was so suicidal as to brave that torrent of crude oil and debris to rescue Moran right that instant.

Nobody except Ki...

—•— WESLEY ELLIS —•—

LONE STAR

AND THE
CALIFORNIA OIL WAR

A JOVE BOOK

LONE STAR AND THE CALIFORNIA OIL WAR

A Jove Book / published by arrangement with
the author

PRINTING HISTORY
Jove edition / November 1985

ISBN: 0-515-08397-6

PRINTED IN THE UNITED STATES OF AMERICA

Chapter 1

"I knew the oil strike meant trouble for us," Miss Alice Ferguson declared, guiding her canopy-top surrey through central Los Angeles. "Was only a matter of time, I told Papa. Now even with you here, I fear there's going to be more and bigger trouble before this blasted business is finished."

"Your father's letter certainly made it sound like something busted loose," Jessica Starbuck responded. "What about your local law?"

"Too much for him. Sheriff Wexler's okay, but he hasn't nearly enough men to police the area. Orange County's pretty darn big and rugged, y'know." The young woman smiled hopefully at Jessie. "That's why I'm so pleased you've come. Only Starbuck ability and prestige can get to the bottom of this and restore our peace."

"Well, we're not magicians, but we'll definitely do all we can." Jessie returned Alice's smile with one of

1

reassurance, but her long-lashed green eyes were emerald-dark with concern—concern not only for the dangerous problem which had drawn her to California, but also for the blind faith, and, therefore, the heavy responsibility that the girl was placing on her. "Isn't that right, Ki?"

"Too much is at stake not to," Ki replied from behind them, his small Gladstone and Jessie's leather bellows case alongside him on the upholstered rear seat. Like Jessie, Ki felt uneasy about Alice's high expectations. True, Jessie was very rich and influential and had the vast resources of her worldwide Starbuck organization to draw upon. But she—and he, too, for that matter—were still flesh and blood, still capable of human error and frailties, still able to be injured, wounded, and killed. Hard work they could promise; miracles they could not.

On the other hand, such fervent belief in the Starbuck reputation seemed to add spirit and confidence that would, Ki hoped, help Alice face any future peril. Not that she wasn't already a resolute gal—her pluck was obvious in the skillful manner she handled the surrey, and in the game way she pushed back her blue sunbonnet from her braided golden hair as she turned to give Ki a smile, too.

In fact, Alice Ferguson cut quite a rambunctious figure. She was young, about eighteen or nineteen, and all of five feet two in her riding boots. Her blue gingham frock clung close to her nubile breasts, enticing thighs, and tapered legs. Her face was aquiline, regular, with perky lips. Her eyes of blue matched her dress and held an audacious, full-of-hell expression that mirrored her youth.

By contrast, Jessie was in her mid-twenties, and though not much older than Alice, she was far more mature. Tall and lissome, she sat with supple yet regal grace, her taut, full breasts thrusting against the light wool bosom

2

of her two-piece beige outfit. Equally stylish was her turban hat, which hid the pinned coils of her copper-blond tresses, but did little to conceal her cameo-shaped face. Pert-nosed, full-mouthed, she exuded her inner core of warmth and passion and courage . . . and, at the moment, she reflected her grave determination to meet and beat this latest threat.

Hers was a lifelong fight, a conflict inherited by her and the rest of the Starbuck empire at the death of her father. Most always it was waged against a wealthy, unscrupulous, international crime cartel, of which Alex Starbuck had run afoul while expanding his career to the Orient. His struggle with this Prussian-based ring, whose aim was to gain control of emerging America through violence and corruption, had led to the murder of his wife, Jessie's mother, and eventually to his own assassination.

But by then his business had evolved into a globe-spanning conglomerate, and his daughter had grown into a shrewd, daring young woman. Using her powerful inheritance and her father's secret records, Jessie continued the battle to destroy every vestige of the criminal conspiracy. And it, in turn, was bent on stopping her. That was why Jessie was discreetly carrying her custom .38 Colt pistol in her jacket, and a two-shot .38 derringer tucked in her dainty chatelaine purse.

It was also why Ki was along. Born of a Japanese woman wedded to an American sailor, Ki had a handsome bronze complexion, almond eyes and straight blue-black hair from his mother's side, and a lean, sinewy body from his father's. Orphaned at an early age, he had apprenticed himself to one of the last samurai, Hirata, who taught him unarmed combat and martial arts. Then, immigrating to America, Ki had been hired by Alex

3

Starbuck and virtually grew up with Jessie on the Starbucks's Circle Star Ranch in Texas. He stayed on after her father's death, a brotherly companion and confidant, ever ready to protect Jessie and her interests. Now in his early thirties, Ki was, to a great extent, the guardian of the throne Jessie wore.

As befit his position, Ki wore a simple dark brown traveling suit. Instead of less comfortable boots, his feet were clad in Asian-style, rope-soled cloth slippers, yet in this land of moccasins and sandals, these didn't cause any undue attention. Sheathed behind his waistband was a short, curved *tanto* knife; and for a belt he used a *surushin*, a six-foot cord with a leather-covered lead ball at each end; and stashed in his vest and pockets were slim throwing daggers and a supply of *shuriken*, little razor-sharp steel disks shaped like six-pointed stars. Ki didn't pack a firearm—he didn't care for them as a rule—but he was anything but defenseless.

Constantly vigilant, Ki surveyed Los Angeles as they drove through to its southern limits. Teeming with a heterogeneous population, the town was infused with a strange, commingling atmosphere of mañana and hurrawin'. The majority of the residents were either Mexican or Californians of Mexican descent. There was a sedateness in the seraped figures moving along the streets that jarred with the raw and brawling vitality of the migrant laborers, railroad workers, and former gold miners who packed the saloons and pleasure dens. The advent of the Southern Pacific, and its introduction of cheap travel to the West and Southwest, had opened up Los Angeles to every man seeking better times and better climes. Opened it up wide.

Jessie and Ki had arrived in Los Angeles the previous day, having taken the Southern Pacific from El Paso.

4

They'd come at the request of Ian Ferguson, general manager of a Starbuck-owned ranch outside Vinada, southeast of Los Angeles. Boiled down, his floridly written letter stated that the depredations of a neighboring rancher, Ramon Cartinas, required immediate curtailing before a range war and the budding oil deal all blew up.

As usual before leaving on such a trip, Jessie researched home-office records and telegraphed her California operatives to investigate the situation. These detectives, along with a confidential notebook that her father had started back when he'd first discovered the cartel, were part of a network to which she'd fallen heir. Continually updated, the book listed detailed information that, added to the detective's work, proved to be invaluable in tracking and eradicating members of the criminal gang.

As it turned out this time, nothing in the notebook, records, and subsequent reports from California indicated that the cartel was involved. It didn't matter. A Starbuck company was in jeopardy at a very crucial point. Jessie knew Ferguson, her father having personally hired him some years ago, and she knew he wouldn't have asked unless he desperately needed help. So help he would get.

So from her Circle Star Ranch, she and Ki had ridden a series of bone-jolting stagecoaches to El Paso, then the iron rattler to Los Angeles, where they'd spend the night recuperating in the "guaranteed softest beds" of the Melrose Hotel. After a dawn breakfast, they'd been picked up by Ferguson's daughter, who was speeding them the thirty-five or so miles to the ranch in time for dinner. Now well en route and leaving Los Angeles behind in roiling plumes of dust, they listened to Alice relate in detail the recent happenings that had set the area on its ear.

"Down here along the coastal valley has its fine points,

5

but not as good cattle range. Up closer around the foot-hills, in the draws and groves, we can raise pretty fair stock, if given enough space," Alice explained. "That's why fences are few and far between. Oh, there're well-established boundaries 'twixt our land and that of our neighbors, but traditionally it's all been kept open country. And that's why we and the other ranchers, Miss Starbuck—"

"Jessie."

"Uh, Jessie—have a chronic running hassle with the Cartinas bunch. Every roundup or gathering, like the one coming up, they argue hard over each maverick and stray. Why, it got so nasty this spring, we had to import three inspectors to settle the calf disputes."

"I know. I saw the bill from the Cattlemen's Association."

"You should've charged Cartinas. It's his fault."

Ki said, "We understand they're original Spanish Land Grant settlers, Alice. Could it be they're feeling squeezed and are resenting the influx of, well, what they see as strange blood?"

"The Cartinas are and they do, Ki, but they don't get along with their own kind any better'n they do us gringos. No, they're a plain prickly lot who rile fast and cool slow." Alice switched her team to a spritely trot, then continued: "We've been and would've kept on handling the cattle and land-line hassles, though, and they're not why Papa sent for you, Miss—Jessie. It was our strip of desert flats that partially borders the Cartinas spread. It was always considered utterly worthless until some four months ago when Mr. Teague came to Papa and made him a proposition, which Papa passed on to you."

"Yes," Mr. Teague was convinced that oil deposits underlay the strip and he wanted to drill," Jessie said, nodding. "Broderick Teague is an absolute expert in geology and petrology. My father hired him fresh out of college, I recall, to do a number of mineral and petroleum surveys, and they became quite good friends. Naturally, his opinion convinced me, so I negotiated a shares agreement. Next thing I heard from him, he'd sunk a well and struck oil."

"Since then six other wells have been brought in, and Mr. Teague's in the process of drilling more. And since then," Alice grimly added, "Cartinas has been threatening us, Papa in particular. If Papa hadn't taken up with Mr. Teague in the first place, they claim, none of this ruckus over oil would've started. Believe me, a bloody war is in the making. Something must be done."

Oil. Already it had created red-hot booms in Ohio, Pennsylvania, Oklahoma, and Texas, attracting hordes of get-rich-quick promoters, real estate schemers, hawkers of questionable trades, and downright thugs, drifters, and owlhoots, all smacking their lips in anticipation of rich pickings. So far such a boom hadn't descended upon California, though there were growing speculations from knowledgeable men, like Broderick Teague, that much of Los Angeles, Orange, and San Diego counties was floating atop promising fields. Perhaps in time, Jessie thought, this region would spark the next California gold rush—a black gold rush.

For the present, however, the southern coastal plain was mostly an unpopulated rubble of low, eroded sandstone hummocks, notched gullies, and pockets of chaparral, eucalyptus, and live oak. Where water could be had for irrigation, there were cornfields, gardens, and orchards. Every so often there would be a village—Bell, Norwalk, La Mirada—each with its clump of weathered frame bungalows and mud-colored adobes blending with

7

the ocher terrain, and a tiny square in which children, dogs, and goats romped freely. The day's heat filtered from the earth in scribbly waves, dancing like film along the crusty hard road, which twisted like a tired, dusty snake southeasterly . . . toward the sparse, humped contours of the San Juan Hills, in whose gulches and canyons many cows fed on scrubby pasture, and at whose base was the Starbuck-owned ranch.

Ki asked, "What exactly is the ruckus about?"

"Various things," Alice replied. "Drillers, riggers, and other oil workers have just about taken over Vinada. It used to be a comfortable and orderly place for the cattlemen, but now Ramon Cartinas swears it's not fit for decent folks, and he'n his wife Ysabelle—wow, is she a spitfire!—won't go there to shop anymore. It's gotten pretty rough, I grant, but they refuse to see that some of it is the price of progress. They don't want progress. They're howlingly convinced that the oil will ruin the cow business, just kill it deader'n a doornail. And lately, there's been violence."

"Any deaths?"

"Almost, Jessie, almost. First the Cartinas foreman, Ev Moran, picked a fight with one of our crew in the Oasis Saloon and plugged him through the shoulder. Papa demanded Moran's arrest, and Sheriff Wexler locked him up till Cartinas came to bail him out, boiling mad. Then somebody set fire to a well and almost burned up some fellows. Rumor blamed Cartinas, said he'd torched the well to get revenge, but he denied it and got furiouser than ever, cursing out Papa."

Alice paused, concentrating on braking the team as the road swerved down a grade toward the bed of the Santa Ana River. Ahead, the road forded the water and ascended the far bank toward an upthrusting hillside of

8

seried rock slabs, briar, and gear grass.

Ki frowned. "Sounds like what happened at Beaumont," he remarked, "when a gas well ran wild and killed a lot of horses and cattle and hogs and three men. Stockmen set that well on fire."

"If they did," Alice observed, shrugging, "they sure didn't poison and rustle their stock, too, I betcha." Again she hesitated, sluffing the wagon across several cutbanks into lower levels of sand before reaching water's edge— an indication of how the waning summer had dried up the river course. She went on, "Anyway, that's the sort of skunk-work the Cartinas are accusing Papa of most recently."

"Total nonsense," Jessie scoffed.

"Of course. Now, I haven't heard it directly from Señor Cartinas, nor has Papa, but we did get an earful from Señora Cartinas about how they're suffering losses and how our oil is spoiling their grass and water and killing their cows. She wouldn't let us on their range to check it out, but I'll say this much, Jessie, we're missing a few extra head than we should be, and we found fifty or so of 'em stretched out cold just the other morning."

"You mean *our* cattle are dying?" Jessie demanded.

"That's right—down on our southwest pasture. Papa says someone must've dumped arsenic into the springs there."

"Someone translated as Señor Cartinas?"

Alice nibbled her lower lip before answering. "I can't think of anybody else who might have reason to, but there's no proof," she said untying the reins from the brake-arm as the horses sloshed out on the other bank. "It's awful easy to point a finger at people you don't like when things start going wrong."

The sound of a shot momentarily deafened them.

9

Jessie's hat flew off as if smitten by some great and invisible hand, and smack dab through her hat's cloth and straw webbing was drilled the burning tunnel of a big-bore slug. Jessie ducked low, unscathed but unnerved; Ki lunged forward to help her; Alice screamed; and the bullet, ricocheting off a metal seat bracket, angled up through the front panel and slashed a bloody furrow along the broad rump of one of the horses. The piercing whinnies of first one, then both, rearing, plunging horses and the raucous clatter of the surrey added to the noisy bedlam. The frenzied animals bolted headlong out of the ford, Alice fighting a set of taut reins that wrenched and jerked like angry snakes in her hands.

They caromed off a large boulder, and Alice tried to avoid the next one by reining sharply. Her panicked team responded to her frantic pull by whirling completely about, ramming into each other, and crashing against the thick root of an overturned tree as they rattled back toward the water. The wild swerve had tilted the surrey dangerously, and Ki fought to balance it with his weight. He felt the wagon lean beyond its center of gravity.

"Jump!" he yelled. "Jump!" Ki felt the seat jerk as Alice released the reins and dived off, Jessie a kick behind her, and then the surrey was tipping over, and he threw himself free.

They struck, tumbling across corrugated stones and gritty sand, and splashed to a sprawling halt in the shallow water. Ki happened to crane a swift glance at the spooked team, and that fleeting shift of his head perhaps saved his life. For with all the shrill cries of the horses and the dragging smashes of the upset surrey, the next gunshot passed unheard. But Ki felt the fiery breath of its bullet fan by, leaving his cheek tingling as he pivoted, alarmed, to warn Jessie and Alice, who were floundering to their feet nearby.

Before he could shout, a third bullet made a sharp splatter into the water next to Alice. No need to shout then—all of them springing in a mad scramble to the bank and burrowing for shelter among its boulders. There they hunched, shivering wet and hugging the dank sand, glimpsing wisps of gunsmoke from a high nitch in the yonder rock slope. Jessie took out her pistol and began wiping it dry.

"I have a carbine," Alice said lamely, "in the surrey."

Ki grinned his thin, feral grin. "It's okay. Our pal is too holed in for anything but the luckiest of shots. Somebody's just got to go up there and root him out. Cover me, Jessie."

She nodded, but there was anxiety in her eyes.

"Can't we simply wait?" Alice pleaded.

"Sure, and so can the ambusher," Jessie answered, watching Ki slip away upriver. "We're on foot and out there's open country. Even waiting till nightfall, we'd be prime targets in the moonlight."

Her pistol lacked the range to hit the ambusher, but Jessie hoped it would focus his attention. It worked, the noisy buck of recoil against her palm each time she shot drawing a barrage of return rifle fire. Beside her, Alice cringed instinctively as thunderous discharges and rock-spanging lead echoed back and forth, while distantly could be heard the horses galloping off, having finally broken free of their harness.

Keeping low to the bank and crawling through a myriad of chunky boulders, Ki wormed his way up around the first big bend in the river. He went a little farther, until he was sure he was beyond the view of the am-

11

busher's rock crevice, then crept onto the rim of the bank and sprinted crouching across a broad sunbaked stretch to the foot of the jumbled stone hillock.

From there he climbed with patient caution, knowing he was within earshot of the ambusher's perch. He avoided crossing gravel and loose shale as much as possible, taking advantage of bare ledges and troughlike depressions, parting scraggly undergrowth carefully and slipping through with hardly a sound. Gradually, implacably shifting higher, he reached a stratum of wind-stunted, big-cone spruce growing near the summit. He paused, glancing briefly through a slight opening in the limbs at the lowering sun, aware of a silence that had dropped with startling abruptness. The faint, sad ripple of water about the overturned surrey was the only sound.

Ki bent his head, tuning his senses to their most sensitive. He waited, breathing softly, until at last he heard a telltale noise—the soft, spitted slap of an ejected stream of tobacco juice.

Between Ki and that chaw of tobacco was a sharp slope, followed by more brush and rock. The stone face of the slope was as slippery as grease, and the slope angled so steeply that Ki had to slither on elbows and knees until he could wedge into the scrub. Ahead loomed a great huddle of conical stones flanking an outward-jutting spur of the hill ridge. Hidden movement on their far side was barely discernible, but it was enough for Ki to zero in on as he snaked through the bushy growth and slid between the tall, cracked rocks.

He bellied in quietly from the left and saw the shadowy outline of a short, thin man lying prone in the spur's clearing. The clearing was V-shaped, the spur like the prow of a ship thrusting out and overlooking the ford in the river and protected on both sides by low-slabbed

12

boulders. Across from Ki, the broad rear of the clearing continued on around the hill to where, he supposed, some sort of trail connected it to the road below.

Up at the apex of the clearing, where there was no stone, the man was stretched out and shouldering a carbine, sighting down at the river bank. Ki recognized the carbine as a .50-caliber Ball, with the magazine under the barrel holding eight rimfire cartridges, loading from the rear. It was a choice piece of killing equipment, and told Ki something about the man using it. What he wanted now was for the man to tell him a lot more about why he was using it.

Problem was, the clearing was layered with pebbly gravel, the kind that crunches underfoot no matter how softly one treads. Ki was not close enough to launch an unarmed attack, and he seriously doubted he could sneak close enough and still catch the man off-guard— and he knew from harsh experience that while martial arts and Ninja tricks have many superior qualities, out-maneuvering a pointblank bullet wasn't one of them. He'd have to bluff the man into surrender.

Ki rose out from the rocks, fingering a couple of *shuriken* just in case. "Not a sound, not a move, you're surrounded," he barked, coldly, walking noisily as though he were wearing big boots. "Give one peep, one twitch, and we'll blow you to smithereens."

The man, flat with his back more or less to Ki, didn't say a word, but he sure moved. Like a scalded ferret he moved, swiveling about and firing as rapidly as he could, having some of the quickest reflexes Ki had ever witnessed outside Japan.

Ironically, he was too swift. He triggered a split-second too soon in his swing and missed, while twisting too fast for Ki to aim a wounding blow accurately. Before the

13

man could squeeze off a properly lined shot, a wrist-flicked *shuriken* spun, slicing deep into his partially exposed chest. The man rolled wailing, the carbine blasted into the air, and blood spewed out like a geyser.

The *shuriken* had inadvertently severed a main artery. Ki ran to the man, cursing his luck. The man just seemed to deflate before his eyes, draining out his life in pumping spurts, then dribbles, then nothing, the ground beneath him becoming a thirsty crimson muck. The man died exceedingly quickly.

Ki moved the carbine aside and hauled the body by the legs to a dry patch. He knew he'd never seen this guy before; he'd have remembered a face as ungodly apelike as his. It had warts and liver spots and squinty little streaks for eyes, the only large thing being a tooth the size of a fat man's thumb that had grown out over the rest of his front teeth. Nor, when searching the pockets of the nondescript clothing, to retrieve his *shuriken*, did he discover anything of significance. The dead ambusher remained a stranger.

Rising, Ki angled to the far rear of the clearing and went around the side of the hill. There, as he'd supposed, was the juncture of a narrow, little used path that dipped winding down the hillside. He also found the ashes of a fire, a rumpled bedroll, a saddlebag store of provisions and ammunition, and a tethered piebald mare placidly cropping weeds. The mare bore a meaningless Mexican brand, and its loose-cinched rig was regulation rangeland gear with no outstanding peculiarities.

His survey completed, Ki untied the horse and was beginning to lead it toward the body when he spotted Jessie and Alice trotting breathlessly up the path. He waved to assure them he was all right, as Jessie called

14

panting: "We heard a gunshot . . . We feared . . ."

"Our friend won't be bothering us anymore," he said. "If you would, Alice, go take a quick peek and see if you know him at all."

The two women hastened on ahead of Ki and looked down at the man's death-contorted face. Alice shuddered, averting her eyes and shaking her head. "Not a bit, so far as I can recall," she replied.

"Too bad. He knew us," Ki said, joining them. *"Of* us, at any rate. He chose this site beforehand and camped here knowing we'd be riding by sooner or later. Damn, I wish I'd taken him alive."

Jessie nodded, her eyes narrowing a trifle. "Well, I know him. I remember his description, that tooth in particular." Her voice was terse, biting, indicating to Ki that the description had been in the notebook she'd studied just prior to the trip. "He's Billy the Buck. A better than average gun-for-hire, frequently for you-know-who."

Alice asked, "Who?"

"Oh, some crooks we chanced across once," Jessie hedged, preferring not to go into detail about the cartel. "That still doesn't explain what the reason was behind Billy the Buck waylaying us."

"I don't like saying this, but . . . Cartinas runs a salty crew, and one of their threats was to hire on more. Maybe they have, worse ones like him," Alice suggested, grimacing at the dead man. "I imagine we should take him in to Sheriff Wexler, shouldn't we?"

For a moment Jessie considered. "It may be best to do nothing. Billy's not wanted by the law, and bringing him in on his horse might hamstring us in legal tangles. It'd surely alert whoever hired him, which'd make it a great deal harder for us. If we keep this quiet, we'll keep free to maneuver and keep our enemies off-balance. Besides, we scarcely owe this treacherous killer much of any consideration."

"Your idea is better than mine, Jessie. I was just going to let his horse carry him wherever, but that could arouse an investigation if'n when he was found, depending on who found him." Ki tied the reins to the saddlehorn and slapped the horse across the rump, sending it galloping on its way. "I agree. Let the law, or Billy the Buck's cronies, find their own dead and solve their own puzzles."

Trying to solve the toughest puzzle of the lot, Jessie thought grimly, as they began to hike down the path to the road. It was a murderous puzzle, and its solution would probably entail death as well. So far she had only one clue: the name Cartinas.

Yet what a name that was! Cartinas could stir talk quicker than most any other name in Southern California, talk that was wild and mixed with impossible tales and apocryphal feats. It was talk of monumental recklessness and unbridled furies, of violent antipathy toward all who had not trekked from Mexico on the heels of Padre Junipero Serra, of three generations of passionate women and ungovernable men, with the deviltry of Satan bred into their blood.

Jessie had already heard fragments of the Cartinas legend when she received Ian Ferguson's letter. When her detective had submitted a more complete report, stating it was hard to determine who Señor and Señora Cartinas hated the worse—Ferguson or the oilmen—he had passed on a warning with it: *You may have a bloody chore on your hands*.

Now blood had already spilled, with promise of more to flow. Her chore still remained, compounded by the puzzle of who had hired Billy the Buck: Was it the cartel? Had Cartinas done so out of personal hatred and a thirst to start a range war? Or had Cartinas and the cartel diabolically joined forces?

And above all, why?

Chapter 2

"If I'm going to have to walk the rest of the way to town," Jessie declared, when they arrived back at the river bank, "I'm going to walk in something drier, cleaner, and more sensible."

Alice, watching Ki retrieve their luggage from where the surrey had first overturned, nodded and sighed. "Vinada's not far, only a few more miles, but I don't blame you." Removing her boots, she padded barefoot to water's edge, hitched her soiled gingham gown knee-high, and was wading toward the wreckage of her wagon as Ki returned with his Gladstone and Jessie's bellows bag.

Jessie went into one set of boulders, Ki into another. When Jessie reappeared, she was wearing a plain silk blouse and form-hugging denim pants and jacket. Her derringer was now concealed behind the wide square buckle of her leather belt, and her pistol was holstered at her thigh. This may not have looked as stylish as her fashionable beige ensemble, but considering what had just occurred, it was eminently more practical. Ki, too, changed into more workaday clothes and was now clad in well-worn jeans, a collarless cotton twill shirt, and, as before, his rope-soled slippers. The weapons from his suit he'd secreted in the many pockets of an old leather vest.

By now Alice had come back from the surrey, clutching a damp Winchester .44-40 carbine, which she'd rescued from beneath the broken front seat. Jessie wanted to carry her repacked bag, but Ki persuaded her not to, citing the need to keep her hands free in case her gun was needed. Then, with her cumbersome bag on one shoulder held steady by one hand, Ki picked up his Gladstone and they all set off up the bank toward the road.

In the flush of a fiery late afternoon, they began their hike to Vinada. They trudged slowly, partly to save energy, partly to use caution. The unexpected ambush had made them wary, alerting them that others knew they were traveling this way, at this time. And considering they were stuck on foot, armed only with Ki's hand weapons, Alice's carbine and wet ammo, and Jessie's close-range shooters, the trio figured that, for now, discretion was the better part of valor.

They reached Vinada without further incident. The sky had evolved to a soft powder-blue enamel, the sun continuing its decline into evening, its slanting rays burnishing the western slopes of the San Juan hills, setting them afire. Closer ahead, in a valley cupped by the foothills, Vinada seemed at first glance to be sleepily ashimmer, logy with heat in the lowering light.

Indeed, as they entered through its outskirts, they saw

that around the characteristic old Spanish plaza were adobe homes shuttered from day's glare and low false-fronted buildings wrapped in growing shadows. Yet fanning out in all directions from this core were the tents and unpainted board structures that showed plainly that Vinada was on a rouser. The few unpaved streets were surprisingly crowded, and there was a bustling air about the place unusual for a cowtown except on pay days.

"The oil strike is creating a boom, okay," Ki mused. "The sort of thing that brings in all sorts of gents, and money, too."

"And I know where they spend it," Alice responded grumpily. "Look at the saloons, at the Oasis there! Like flies on a ham bone!"

"Speaking of ham, I could use a break," Jessie said, pausing with fatigue. "I know we're late, and your father'll be waiting with dinner, Alice, but I could certainly use a snack, something cold to drink, and a chair to sit down in before we go on. Any suggestions?"

"The Top Hat, next to the Oasis," Alice replied, nodding agreement. "The food is passable, especially for quick bites."

They crossed the plaza, passed the noisy Oasis, and went in the Top Hat. The restaurant was a large, square room, the hubbub from the saloon echoing through their common wall and adding to the loud talk of patrons at its stubby tables and a short rear bar.

Most of the customers were brawny men in breeches, boots, and flannel shirts, many with pistols sagging in holsters. These, Ki decided as they took an empty table, were oil workers, doubtless from the night shift, but there was more than sprinkling of cowhands. There were also quite a few gentlemen wearing the homely garb of the rangeland, yet their hands, Ki felt sure, were not marred

20

by marks of rope or branding iron.

A paunchy man in a bib apron and dungarees came out from the back, scratching his hairy chest through the sides of his apron. Jessie ordered three roast beef sandwiches and coffee, the sandwiches and brew being standbys that most cafes would have fresh on hand. Shortly the man returned with their food, and Jessie paid him.

They ate hungrily. After they'd finished, Alice stretched in her chair, gave a dainty little hiccup, and said, "I feel like a new lady. If you're ready, let's hire a rig at the livery and be on our way before Papa sends the troops out searching for us."

Ki hesitated before rising. "Jessie, d'you think we ought to first try'n see Broderick Teague? He's got an office here, doesn't he?"

"Well, his address is in Vinada," she answered. "Father trusted him, I feel. And he didn't trust many, so I believe we can trust him, too, as a friend as well as business associate. Frankly, though, I doubt he knows more about the violence than the Fergusons do already. Yes, I plan to visit him soon as possible, but to delay leaving in order to visit right now . . ." Jessie broke off with a shrug.

"True, true. It was just an idea brought on by oil being the sort to attract all sorts," Ki said, repeating his former rumination while casually gazing around. "I've a notion that some of these gents do most of their riding between sunset and sunrise."

"Where's the connection?" Alice asked, slightly impatient. "Assuming they're all robbers and rustlers, I don't see what they could hope to gain by causing big trouble for us or Mr. Teague."

"Land values go down when such things happen and land is easier to buy," Ki observed. "Even oil land, which normally goes sky-high."

"That's so," Alice allowed. "But Mr. Teague says the prime drilling is out on the sands, and that whole strip is already owned by us—I mean by you, Jessie, and you're not the kind to cave in to pressure. So don't you think, Ki, your idea is a bit farfetched?"

"Probably. Still, in a situation like this, we can't afford to overlook any bets, no matter how slim or against the odds."

Jessie nodded thoughtfully. "You've got a point, Ki. We'd better look up Broderick Teague, if he's here in town."

"Oh, very well, I'll take you. His office is in the ground floor of his home," Alice explained and turned on her heel. She glanced over her shoulder. "How about it, are you coming or not?"

They left the restaurant, shouldered past the plaza turmoil, and angled along dusty sidestreets toward the northern edge of town. At last they came to what was patently the most imposing structure in Vinada, a two-story, whitewashed house done in a pseudo-mission style with a gabled slate roof, a colonnaded front porch, and a latticed porte-cochere on the left side, through which a crushed-shell drive went to a rear yard. From the front door to the left side, there were two small windows and another door, this one adorned with B. TEAGUE & CO. in gilt lettering.

"Looks like friend Broderick has managed very nicely for himself," Ki remarked, sizing up the place as they approached the door.

"He just finished having it built," Alice said and began to enter, adding cattily, "Be careful. The paint may still be wet."

Inside the incongruously plain, sparsely furnished

room, they saw a hulking towheaded bruiser of a man hunched over a sturdy desk. He was studying a spread of cards before him and raised a clearly disinterested eye. His glance acquired a contemptuous gleam at the sight of Jessie and Ki's simple garb and Alice's bedraggled clothes.

"You got no business here," he growled, his eyes resuming their scrutiny of the cards. "The boss just deals with oilfield muckers, not with no women or Chinks. Move along."

"I think Teague will want to see us," Ki replied calmly, setting the baggage down, as Jessie and Alice stood fuming. "These two ladies are friends of his."

"G'wan!" The man's thick lips twisted in a disgusted smirk, his tone insinuating deep insult. "The boss's lady friends don't come a-callin' in twosomes, dragging their laundryman along with them."

Ki remained outwardly unperturbed, smiling thinly now, aware of Jessie bristling beside him. "Maybe if that's the way of it, then perhaps I should have said Miss Starbuck here is a family friend."

"Out!" There was great annoyance in the man's murky eye as he straightened from his chair. To Ki it was apparent that talking would mean nothing to this watchdog. His was the type of simple, one-track mind that once given orders would obey them regardless. "Out, the pack o' you, or am I gonna have to bounce you out on your—"

"No," Ki purred. And reaching, Ki had him by the shirt and half-dragged across the desk so fast that the man scarcely had time to blink in disbelief and dismay. Then Ki's hand, flat and open-palmed, sledged into his whisker-stubbled jaw, reversing his unwilling direction

23

and slamming him back so hard that his big bulldog head drummed against the wall behind him with a reverberating thud.

An inner door near the desk popped open, and a dark-suited, dark-haired man of a height about equal to Jessie's burst out. Even in anger he had a dandified air of importance and a cock's stance.

"What gives here?" he demanded in a surprisingly resonant voice, after first glimpsing the man who had slumped groggily against the wall. Then sight of the two women aroused a faltering gasp, "Why, Miss Ferguson! Alice! And m'gawd, you're, aren't you Jes—"

The rest of his question was lost as the man, recovering with an outraged bellow, launched from the wall. Perhaps desperate to recover himself in the eyes of his employer, he closed upon Ki with startling speed for one who appeared so muscle-bound and ungainly. Charging with chin hugging his chest and ham-like hands doubled into massive fists, the man was a two-legged bull closing for the kill.

But Ki sidestepped lightly, one hand snatching one of the room's chairs by its solid wood back. Snapping it over his shoulder, Ki brought the chair down across the back of the man's head and neck in a quick, splintering blow before the man could ward it off. The man dropped like a collapsing sack, the parquet floor trembling as his bulk crashed upon it. The fractured shambles of the chair littered his back and the floor beside him.

The primly tailored little man in the doorway gaped, his brown eyes widening with wonder. But it was Jessie's cool voice that sounded upon the heels of the crash. "Ki, you remember Broderick Teague, don't you? I certainly do. How are you, Broderick?"

Teague, shaking himself as from a daze, rushed forward. "You can't be," he marveled, his small, manicured right hand outstretched eagerly. "But you are, as I live and breathe! Jessica Starbuck! I haven't seen you since before your father, ah, passed away. My, you don't look at all like the—like the—young girl I last met."

"Taking on plans and responsibilities has a way of growing a child up fast," Jessie responded soberly. She clasped his hand in a firm grip and shook it businesslike, instead of letting him raise it to his lips as he had plainly intended. "We've all changed with age, Broderick. Ki has, don't you agree? You do recall him."

"Yes, yes, of course." Teague smiled perfunctorily at Ki, then shifted his gaze to Alice. "Heavens, something sure happened to you! You're going to give poor Ian a conniption fit when you answer to him."

"Papa's hired to herd cows, not me," Alice retorted tartly.

Teague chuckled, his eyes appraising her pleasantly and without offense. Turning, he glanced at the unconscious man and commented, "Whitey will be fine there." Then he gestured toward the inner door. "Come on in my office, where we can talk."

When the door was closed behind them and the three guests were each seated in one of the luxurious chairs that graced his office, Teague settled at his ornate executive desk and stated, "Something must have happened, else you wouldn't be here, Jessica."

"Something has." While she related a brief account of the problems leading up to and including the ambush, Jessie took mental note of how Teague had changed with age. From a young man in disheveled field khakis, he'd grown to be an elegant dresser, his broadcloth suit and checked waistcoat perfectly fitted, a pure-white stock filling the gap at his throat. He'd become vain—with reason so far as his figure was concerned. Yet at some time he'd suffered from smallpox or an injury, and this had left his face pocked. To hide the scars, Teague sported a neatly trimmed beard; it jerked pointedly when Jessie finished and he thrust his chin forward, his deep-set eyes piercing and analytical as he pondered her explanation.

"Serious, exceedingly serious," he murmured.

"It appears to me to be all part of an organized opposition," Jessie continued, "possibly the same one providing the hassles you're experiencing, Broderick, here in town and out at the oilfield."

"I suspect, not, Jessica. The only organizing I've heard of is by the Cartinas, who've been trying to use us, the oil, as one excuse to whip up resentment against the Fergusons—your ranch, that is. Why they want you to pull stakes—well, your guess is as good as mine."

"You've got it backwards, Mr. Teague," Alice countered. "Cartinas is for open range and fears your wells mean ditches, pipelines, bad smells, and cattle poisoned by gas and oil slicks."

"They're wrong, Alice. The strikes are the best thing that ever happened to this section, bringing in new people and good fortune."

"Precisely what they're scared of," she argued. "They want it like it was and want for you oilmen, not us ranchers, to leave here."

"Then they're in for disappointment," Teague said with a grin. "A huge pool lies just beneath the entire length of desert crust. It has to; the natural slope of the beds all flow toward that burned-out stretch of Hades. I'm in hock to my elbows from buying more equipment, and I'm going to stay here drilling as long as my contract allows."

"Or until you pump it dry?"

"I couldn't, Jessica, not in two lifetimes. But oil aside, in my opinion you're up against a vicious row 'tween Spanish and Anglo ranchers. They never did get along and likely never will."

"No reason they can't, though," Ki said. "All it takes is for both sides to temper down and try a little common sense."

"And that's what haughty, obstinate firebrands like Ramon and Ysabelle Cartinas cannot seem to do," Teague replied, furrowing his brow. "You know how I run my operations, Jessica. Strict as the devil on rules. No mixing in local feuds. But I don't slack on precautions, either, and I keep my boys armed on the job and prepped for trouble. I'll have them pay closer watch on the Cartinas crew, and I'll do whatever I can for you. What are your plans, Jessica?"

"I haven't made any, not just yet," she answered. "We have to get to the ranch and talk with Ian, and then we'll decide."

"Since you're staying there, I won't suggest you use my home as your headquarters, though you're certainly welcome to. But please, let me take you to your ranch. It's a mere jog from the oil wells, and I was about ready to go on my evening check of them anyway."

Teague's offer was promptly accepted with profuse thanks. He rose, smiling again, clapped a soft hat rakishly on his head, and led them into the outer room. The man called Whitey was now sitting in the midst of the fragmented chair, where he had lain. He was still woozy, unable to focus on his dapper little employer.

"Mind the store," Teague said, walking past.

Ki reclaimed the baggage and caught up with Teague. "Sorry about smashing your chair," he said, nodding back toward the man. "Seeing as there was a disagreement, I figured the quicker we straightened it out, the better. It was hard on the chair, though."

Teague shrugged. "Whitey is good in his way, but he's a bit slow when he's faced with the unexpected. Lessons come hard for him." With that, he dismissed the plight of his fallen receptionist.

They went into the house proper and exited through a side door under the porte-cochere. Then they headed down the drive to the stable, where Teague rousted his hostler. The hostler, abjectly apologetic, told him the three-seat platform wagon he wanted was apart with a busted spring shackle. So Teague, throttling his irritation, assured his guests that although he hadn't a suitable wagon to carry them in, he had a plentiful stock of saddle horses and gear to choose from, which they could return at their leisure.

Shortly, with Jessie and Ki on chestnut geldings, Alice on a dapple mare, and Teague on a roan stallion almost too large for him, they rode out of the yard and headed easterly toward the hills.

Chapter 3

An hour later, deep inside Starbuck territory, the four riders came to a fork in the ranch's private road. Ahead, the main route bridged a narrow culvert and continued east. The other cut south; though much newer, it showed greater use, its trailbed rutted and blackened from the heavy passage of oil-laden tanker wagons.

Teague signaled to rein in by the fork, then said, "Under that bridge runs the water pipe for my wellhead pumps, Jessica. I had one of your creeks tapped to flow down through there."

"Yes, I remember you writing for permission to."

"I had to go higher up than I wished to find a good source. Your lower springs are apt to be too salty, which plays havoc with steam engines." Teague smiled plumply. "On the other hand, that salt water helped tip me to the oil. Another sign was this scatter of hills hereabouts. Have you noticed how oddly stratified they are?"

"No, I'm afraid not," Jessie admitted. Nor could she now, twilight blurring details as her gaze swept the surrounding terrain.

To her left were canyon thickets and low brushy slopes whose southern base they had been skirting for some time. Ahead were more hills owned by her, loftier and misty purple against the cobalt sky. Her range also extended to the south, but only for a relatively short distance. A line of similar craggy hills less than two miles away belonged to Cartinas.

Immediately on her right, however, the view was very different. Just a few yards from where she sat asaddle, the cap rock abruptly ended, the scrub and stone pastureland giving way to a steep slide of rubble and debris that tumbled to the edge of stark desolation. For roughly a mile in width and seven in length lay desert sand, gray dust, and naked rock, forming a great arid trough that separated her grazing land from Cartinas's north boundary.

"The rimrock of these hills was once the shore line of a big lake or inland sea," Teague went on to explain, "with conditions perfect for the formation of oil deposits. If you look, you'll find evidence of plant and animal life that flourished here eons ago."

"Not before I look at dinner and a bath," Alice interjected.

"Sorry, I know you're eager to get home. C'mon, it's faster by way of the field—now with the road in—than to continue on up here."

The riders turned their mounts onto the southern fork, and soon they were moving down and out along the desert floor. Jessie felt thankful that it was evening, for during the day, she was sure, this heat-seared basin must shimmer like the top of a raging hot stove. The only vegetation was sparse sage, cactus, and snake-armed ocotillo, clumped meagerly on a corrugated wasteland of shallow erosions and isolated mounds of boulders that looked like nature's tombstones to ages long dead.

Other monuments were set by man. The first to appear was the water pipe, plunging from the culvert at the crest of the embankment, then angling to more or less flank the road. Its fat tubular sections weaved through furrowed ditches, spanned depressions on spindly trestles, and hugged rocky outcrops of iron suspension brackets. Then after awhile they could see the lampglow from clustered tents and shanties, a cook shack, and a few tool and maintenance sheds. Near them was a large, canvas-shaded corral of horses and a number of parked, empty tanker wagons.

Not far beyond were the spires of two seventy-foot wooden derricks. One was being dismantled, the well-head apparently capped. The other was in the process of drilling, the walking beam on top drawing the suspension cable up and down, pounding the heavy steel bit deeper underground. Despite the distance, the rig's muffled, earth-sundering hammer could be heard vibrating from its core.

Spaced about were seven producing wells. Their derricks removed for use elsewhere, displacement pumps chugged and echoed noisily from their remaining platforms. The baffle plates of their valves were open just enough to relieve gas pressure and to feed oil to spigot pipes or into sumps that resembled tarry, black lakes.

As they progressed through the field, Teague gestured toward some large storage tanks under construction. "My latest project, so I can dry up those messy sumps," he said. "Later I aim to build a conduit to the nearest rail-head, if and when the California Southern gets around to laying track this far north."

"That'll be an expensive task."

"Sure will, Jessie, and what with installing pump stations and such, a lot of the cost depends on where the C.S. heads. It's already running from National City through San Diego and up to San Clemente, but can't seem to decide to cross the San Joaquin Hills along the coast or on an inland jog. Whichever way, I'll go to it."

Jessie nodded thoughtfully, the hard resolve in his tone and manner confirming her opinion of him as a determined, ambitious man.

Suddenly Teague cocked his head in an attitude of listening. The rhythmic thud coming from the drilling rig's bore had changed to an erratic punching, and the cable was dancing and quivering.

"Rock," Teague growled, and veered toward the derrick. "Rig must've gotten through that sand bank and hit rock again. They'll probably shut it down now to change the bit and sink new casings."

His estimate proved true. The walking beam slowed and stopped its nodding, the cable ceased jiggling, and the platform crew began to haul out and unscrew lengths of drill stem from the wellhole.

The workers were like others seen here and in town— stalwart of body and having a weathered grimness. Both Jessie and Ki observed how efficient and experienced they were, indicating they were from existing fields back East, displaced and different out West, of a breed already inclined to stick together and not mix with outsiders. It implied that in a local showdown, a range war, they'd refuse to take sides, even if choosing meant saving the very Starbuck whose land they were milking.

Yet when the riders drew close, a couple of men broke from the platform and hurriedly approached, hailing them.

The taller wore range garb and a high-crowned Stetson, his lean hips and long legs carrying him swifter than the second man could trot. That man was barrel-chested and bull-thighed in a stained tan shirt, twill pants, and engineer boots, and though bald, had a wide mattress of a beard spreading down his hefty chest.

Alice cried, "Papa!" and spurred forward.

The tall man quickened his pace as he shoved back his Stetson, displaying an unruly mop of auburn hair. "By gadfry, I found you!"

"I was never lost!" Laughing, Alice reined alongside and flung her arms around him, their hug drawing her from the saddle.

"Gal, I was just chancin' to check thisaway before goin' off to search in earnest. Darn luck I did. Where've you been?"

"It's a long story that can wait. Everything's all right, Papa. Can't you ever let me go anyplace without worrying to a frazzle?"

His answer was another embrace. Released, Alice belatedly remembered her companions, who by now had dismounted to gather near, and while fussing with her clothes, she introduced them to her father.

Ian Ferguson was about the age of Teague, no more than ten years older than Jessie. He'd married early, become a widower early, and was raising his only child alone—which, Jessie thought, might account for his seeming overprotectiveness. Otherwise, he was typical of Starbuck managers; strong, intelligent, honest and hard-working, though occasionally domineering, with his own prejudices and passions.

Why Ferguson hadn't remarried was a puzzle, for he was still youthful, a solid provider, and handsome in a craggy way. His nose was lopsided, and one ear was cauliflowered, evidently from some accurate fists in the past, and his mouth was a generous slash cut for good humor. It quirked pleasantly when he nodded to Ki, but as Jessie's name was given, it lost its amusement, and so did his appealing hazel eyes. She was his boss and not here for fun.

"Thanks for comin', Miss Starbuck. I apologize and take full responsibility for allowin' things to slip so bad outta hand here."

"Please call me Jessie," she replied, hoping informality would ease his strain. "And don't blame yourself for faults not your own, Ian. I'm sure you've done your best. Father always claimed your best *was* the best, especially after you and he set up the ranch operation."

"He spoke about back then, did he?" Ferguson rubbed his jaw. "Did he tell of the time him'n me held off a whole dozen banditos?"

Jessie nodded, face deadpan. "He said he was caught on a barb wire fence and couldn't run, while you had your gun snagged in your gallusses and were forced to shoot through your trouser fly."

Ferguson looked in imminent danger of exploding. Suddenly he relaxed, however, and his anxiety dissolved into hearty laughter.

Teague grabbed that moment to introduce the stocky man as Vince Handstad, foreman of the drillers. Then he pointed at the derrick that was being disassembled. "The well there blew in day before yesterday, and Vince was telling me it's proving another winner."

"Yeah, and like the rest of 'em, Chief, it'll take pumping," Handstad said. "This's the screwiest field I ever worked. First off, I'd have swore there's gas pressure to keep 'em gushing natural, but real soon they peter out. I can't figure it."

"I can't either, Vince, but it's nothing serious. The flows are all good enough to make money. Ah, here comes some riders."

Everyone gazed southward across the gray expanse of desert, surveying a cloud of dust boiling steadily toward them.

"A few of the Cartinas boys, I reckon," Ferguson declared. "Those hellions plumb believe in larrupin' hide wherever they go."

Moments later two riders materialized under the dust cloud. Ki, along with the others, studied the approaching pair gallop in and wrench to a sliding, grit-spewing halt before them.

One was a man who was cut in the same pattern as most good foreman and top hands. Pug-faced, with a muscled body larger and heavier than the average puncher, he regarded his hosts with uncompromising eyes and an air of tough, sure competence. Yet Ki brushed over him, for the man's companion was much more compelling.

The companion was a woman. Ki judged her to be a little past thirty—as was he—and though no ravishing beauty, she projected a presence which piqued his interest. She was dressed in worn range gear, except for a fancy blouse with a lot of Mexican needlework that accentuated her full-breasted, somewhat tall and angular figure. Her features weren't perfectly regular, her nose being a bit long and her chin a bit clipped; yet from her sombrero spilled luxuriant raven hair, which went well with eyes of onyx, devilishly bright. And when she flashed her sharp, pearly teeth in a mockery of a smile, Ki got the idea she would like to sink them in their throats.

Like Ki, Jessie measured the man as in this woman's employ. The woman was more perturbing; Jessie sensed in her a spirit of frustrated power and unrelenting defensiveness, as if, restless and antagonistic, she owed the world a fight and lived only with trouble.

Her impressions were verified when Ferguson nodded curtly to the man and greeted the woman, *"Buenas tardes, Señora Cartinas."*

"Don't good afternoon me, Ferguson. I'm here for one reason, one message. Our property is now posted. Stay clear of it."

Ferguson grew less cordial. "Sounds more like a threat."

"A warning, but take it as you wish. We're gathering a herd to drive through the hills to San Clemente. A railroad stock buyer came to us because the trainyard there is expanding and adding many new workers, and he needs plenty of beef *rápido*. So we're combing our range for every maverick and a stray and don't want interference."

"That's great news," Ferguson declared, beaming amiably and ignoring the startled glances shot his way. "It means the railroad is gearing to start construction. And then it'll really be great when tracks get laid up far enough to where we can ship on it."

"Then it would do away with a very nasty drive," she grudgingly allowed, then caught herself. "But at the rate our cows are going now, there won't be any left by then to ship. Our losses from rustling—and from sickness and death spread by these infernal wells—have made us badly understocked and pressed for funds. That's why now I'm taking drastic steps. The railroad needs our beef, we need their money, and you and your crew need to keep off my land. *Entiende?*"

Jessie understood, and provoked she replied in a cool, acerbic tone, "We're not on Cartinas land. This's Starbuck

36

land, recorded by deed. *My* land, and I have the say who can be here and who cannot."

"Ah, Señorita Starbuck, I have heard of you—who has not?" Her voice was pitched with the recklessness of her spirit. "I am Annamarie Flores Rosarita Ysabelle Cartinas. We Cartinas were here before there were any property laws—before there were any laws at all. The Cartinas grant was secured with guns and it will live by guns. If you haven't heard of it already, you soon will. Cartinas will tolerate no neighbors—"

She broke off in mid-sentence, distracted. They all were—at first feeling rather than hearing—a vague rumbling down in the earth. Mild as it was, the faraway tremor turned the quiet routine on the platform into one of industrious frenzy. And as though panic-stricken, Teague and Handstad bolted for the derrick, the foreman yelling through cupped hands, "Out with the drill stem! Out with the rest of it, and put a valve on that hole!"

Ferguson sidled close to Jessie, using the momentary ferment to murmur. "We'll take a stock tally next coupla weeks. I've a hunch that'll tell you why Cartinas doesn't want any close neighbors."

Ferguson wasn't quiet enough. The man on horseback abruptly shifted and leaned to glare at him. "I heard that! Well, for one thing, you're a damn insinuatin' lizard of a liar. For another—"

"You'll have to make it stronger than that," Ferguson cut in sharply, as Ysabelle Cartinas focused on him, too. "And I'll give you another thing. This morning, thirty more 'o my head were found dead 'round a spring due east o' here, near your line. The pool there had been doctored with arsenic, Moran, with tracks goin' south."

Jessie, recalling Alice's earlier conversation, now tagged the man as the Cartinas segundo. Ev Moran's face

37

bloated ruddy, but it was Ysabelle who reacted out loud. Staring astounded, she gasped, "Do you—do you even dare to suspect us of poisoning your cattle?"

Ferguson shrugged. "I ain't sayin' you personally had a part in it. But doubtless your hands ain't in too sweet a temper over your missin' and dyin' stock. Perhaps they feel justified in retaliating in kind, but my advice is, it's liable to backfire on 'em."

"Your advice ain't worth a damn," Moran said. "You stay away from our land or I'll beat your dirty damn face in."

"Maybe you'd like to try that now," Ferguson challenged.

And Moran began to move as if preparing to dismount.

And Ki figured it was time to step in. Snapping, "No more, not here," he was starting between them when the earth came alive again.

The attack was brief, but its gutteral rumble seemed louder and nearer, its gentle quiver underfoot more distinct and pulsing. Momentarily apprehensive, they eyed the platform and were relieved to see the crew remaining frantically at work. Ysabelle kept stroking her Morgan, soothing it through a case of jitters. Ev Moran had a livelier tussle, his wild-eyed dun snorting and prancing skittishly.

As the spasm faded and the desert grew placid, Ferguson said ruefully, "Thanks, Ki, you're right. I almost got carried away."

"Forget it."

"I ain't." Moran, his horse under control again, began to swing from his saddle. "You're gonna get carried away yet, Ferguson, and so's your yeller pal if he tries—"

He was silenced by the earth, whose crust started literally to shake. Renewed rumblings suddenly intensified, building to a growlish roar and augmented by a weirdly sibilent hissing. And this time they saw Teague, Handstad, and the crew fleeing the rig.

"Run!" Ferguson shouted. "That sucker's gonna blow!"

Grabbing his daughter by the hand, Ferguson launched into a run, Jessie and Ki a lope behind. In back of them, crewmen were fanning out over the desert, direction unimportant so long as it was away from the unleashed forces rushing up perhaps to destroy them.

The quaking pandemonium was too much for Cartinas's horses. Ysabelle's Morgan needed no spurred goadings, but spooked into its own pell-mell gallop southward. Ysabelle went along for the ride.

Ev Moran's hysterical dun erupted in a prime exhibition of buck and wing, sunfishing, pinwheeling, and four-legged flings that got nowhere, but got it there fast. The men racing nearby yelled frantic warnings, but Moran was too busy to hear or heed, clinging perversely, and unable to bring his boogered horse to its senses.

The roar grew thunderous, until with a deafening explosion, tons of pipe were expelled up through the rig floor, blasting upward like enormous chunks of shrapnel. The derrick shattered, while from the wellhole, a hissing black column volcanoed heavenward. The geyser soared to an apex, spread out, then broke. An oily cloudburst fell in a wide ring about the platform, enveloping the cycloning horse and rider, who immediately disappeared from view.

At a safe distance, the crewmen shouted their alarm, aware of the broken iron and timber flying hidden in the downpour. Given a few minutes for the worst to settle, they'd return to try capping the well. But nobody was so suicidal as to brave that torrent of crude oil and debris to rescue Moran right that instant.

Nobody except Ki.

He told Jessie what he was going to do while stripping down to his jeans, and she was appalled. He went anyway, ignoring her protests and the startled cries of the workers as he dashed barefoot back toward the runaway gusher.

It wasn't that Ki felt particularly noble or any affection for that belligerent foreman. His motives were ulterior. A Starbuck aiding a Cartinas would help dispel the antagonisms between the quarreling neighbors—assuring, of course, the clan was not as villainous as dark legend and suspicion painted them. Even if they were, a Starbuck beating the oilmen at their own game would earn their respect and, perhaps, their support in case of a showdown. That is, if he succeeded. If he failed, well . . .

Plunging into the murky rain of oil, Ki thrust for the spot where the figures had vanished. He slogged and slid, quickly becoming as slick-soaked as the ground and finally perceiving man and horse dimly through the drenching spray. Moran was still tucked to the saddle, evidently hoping to outlast the dun until he could regain control—and to outlive it, for though the dun was tiring, it was now slipping perilously with every whirling jump it made.

Ki approached, trying to gauge a pattern to the horse's buck-jerking madness. Moran squinted at him, frowning as if perplexed by Ki's unexpected appearance and dubious about it to boot. Ki didn't make the mistake of calling back, knowing Moran wouldn't hear him above the cascading din and unwilling to swallow an open mouthful of oil for nothing. Instead, he made another mistake.

When he closed within reach, Ki sprang groping for

40

the halter, thinking to slow and steady the horse so Moran could dismount. The horse resisted with a violent wrench that broke Ki's tenuous grip and half unseated Moran. And Moran, whiplashed and teetering, apparently figured Ki was trying sneakily to arrange his fall, so he'd snap his neck or get trampled underfoot. Already enraged, the incensed Cartinas's foreman catapulated the rest of the way out of his saddle, directly at his supposed attacker.

The headlong dive caught Ki unaware, and Moran cannonaded into the easy target of his body. It was a brutal, hurting slam that took Ki down flat. Ki took Moran with him, striking the ground like an octopus wrapped around a windmill, all knees and elbows and gouging hands striving for leverage.

Then, abruptly, Moran was snatched loose and staggering backward, his right arm stretching ungainly behind him. He'd forgotten in his angry haste to release the reins, which he'd wrapped rodeo-style around his wrist, and now the dun was dragging him as it continued leaping rambunctiously. Stumbling, Moran swore wrathfully as he wrestled to stay upright and untangle himself.

That gave Ki the chance to get to his feet, though gasping and winded. He stepped to help, saying, "Listen, I came to—"

"Fuck you, you squint-eyed shit bastard!" Moran raged, dropping the reins, and rushed with a hard one-two combination.

And that crystallized the slow resentment which had been seething in Ki since Moran and Ysabelle had arrived with their arrogant threats and veiled accusations. Blocking Moran's left-right punches with his forearms, he twisted on one foot and snapped out with his other in a *yoko-geri-keage* side-thrust kick. Such a blow could be fatal, but he tempered its force, not wishing to kill Moran but only to stop him, and maybe whump him down a peg or two.

He managed even less than that. His pivoting foot slid a fraction and threw off his aim, his kick skimming along Moran's ribs, causing him to backpedal wavering but unharmed. Ki moved after, irked by the realization that kicks would be useless here, his balance too precarious on ground like slimy, black ice.

Moran kept backing, bumping against his crazily dancing, skating horse and lurching sideward to avoid it as well as Ki. Angling, closing in, Ki struck out with *shuto* strokes—blows with the edge of the hand—his right looping upward from the side, and his left slicing down like a guillotine blade. Retreating faster, Moran proved as good at fighting as his appearance and bullying confidence had indicated, warding off the worst of the punishing slashes, absorbing what he couldn't, stubbornly trying to feint and counter with hammering fists.

Both men were sopping wet, their eyes burning and throats choking from the noxious gasses mixed with the spewing oil. Ki felt his energy flagging, but saw Moran was weakening quickly under his pressuring onslaught and pushed his advantage when he glimpsed an opening. He lanced stiffened fingers at Moran's midriff, his spearhead stab meant to paralyze the man's abdomen and incapacitate him. It would have if it had struck, but at that second Moran stepped in a pool of slippery muck. His feet shot out from under him and he reeled backward over a pile of casing.

Ki, overextended from his thrust, slewed to one knee. And the horse kicked him. His vision blurred and his brain spun, the gusher and its noises growing vague and distorted. Again Ki went down. Before he could roll over and collect himself, Moran was coming at him. This time the foreman held a murderous weapon in his hand—a short length of one inch steel cable.

Moran was swinging it like a club, and Ki knew he was staring at death. That steel cable could split his skull like a ripe melon, or crush an arm if he fended the blow. He was flat and still ringy and hadn't time to fumble for the few sticky weapons his pants carried. He hadn't time to think. Only to react. As Moran rushed, Ki raised both feet close to his chest, then let go with piston driving force. His callused bare heels caught Moran in the groin and sent him howling in pain, the lashing cable end striking harmlessly a scant couple of inches from Ki's head.

Rolling, Ki grabbed the cable before Moran could withdraw it and gave it a savage yank while he scrambled upright. Moran blundered forward from the impetus, the cable ripping from his grasp. Ki flung it aside, noting peripherally that the feckless horse had romped off. Then he stomped down hard on Moran's boots, anchoring him to the sodden ground to keep him where he wanted him, within range.

Ki chopped his right hand at the left side of Moran's neck. Moran writhed; his breath sharpened to a harsh whistle. Ki gave him no more time to recover than Moran had given him, knifing with the stiff edge of his palms on the right neck and across the throat.

He stepped back. Moran sagged limply. Propping the gagging, unresisting man up by one shoulder, Ki slowly, patiently walked him out of the monsoon of oil, back toward the waiting group beyond.

As a rescue, it was a stinker.

A ragged cheer rose, some of the crewmen hastening to congratulate Ki, ribbing his and Moran's soiled ap-

pearance. Ki wiped the smeary oil from his face to clear
his vision and saw that among those gathering were the
Fergusons, Teague, Handstad, and Jessie. Also along was
Ysabelle Cartinas, relief plain on her features. She was
on horseback, having controlled her Morgan and, Ki
guessed, returning out of concern for her foreman; and
she was leading Moran's tuckered dun by its reins, apparently having caught it afield after it had bolted from
the gusher.

Moran, recovering somewhat, showed his apprecia-
tion by shoving Ki and tottered to his now compliant
dun, clenching his fists and swearing foully. He tried to
mount, but was thwarted by his weakened condition and
by the oil coating him, his horse, and his gear. Slipping
and slopping, his comical attempts and blistering frus-
tration were too much for the crewmen's rough humor.
They laughed and poked fun at his antics. And the more
they howled and hooted derisively, the more infuriated
Moran became.

Eventually Moran managed to crawl up over his greasy
saddle and hang like a sack of feed. Then he shifted
upright to settle properly in his hull, cursing all and
sundry and vowing vengeance on Ki.

"Tweren't for the goop in my gunbarrel, I'd have shot
you! I will f'sure next time! Nobody makes an ass outta
me and lives!"

Ki shrugged. "Then shoot yourself, 'cause you did it
to yourself." He turned to Ysabelle. "Sorry, ma'am, I
didn't want to fight."

"Don't think this's an example of Cartinas warring.
Cartinas runs the toughest crew." Hardness now sheeted
over the femininity of her face. "Stay off our land. If
you don't, you'll have your fight."

The *señora* spurred for home. Moran sided her, still ranting, a coal-black rider rocking and sliding aboard a coal-black horse.

Ki watched the pair depart, his grin like that of a stealthy cougar. So, too, did Jessie, her eyes seeming ready to burst afire. Alice and her father stood glowering, and Teague and Handstad looked embarrassed, as if witnesses to a wrangle that didn't involve them.

The crewmen slapped their thighs and bellowed with laughter. "Did . . . did you ever see a dun change color the way his did?" one driller finally gasped, and another cackled, "Boy, were they burnin'!"

Teague wasn't amused. "Shut up and start capping that well!"

"The gas pressure ain't holding full," Handstad remarked. "Wouldn't be surprised if we have to pump before long, but at least it'll be easier to tame now," he added and began bawling orders.

"I notion it's time we left, too," Ferguson said. "Let's get to the ranch, where Ki can clean up and we can tie on the feedbag."

The four collected their horses, and Teague supplied Ki a large strip of packing cloth to drape across his saddle to protect it from Ki's oil-soaked pants, while Jessie kept charge of the rest of Ki's clothes. They set off east across the sands, as the crew started toiling over the gigantic task of capping the gusher.

Ferguson chuckled. "So it's happened."

"A lot has," Jessie replied. "What in particular?"

"You met the she-devil of the Cartinas. And that's not all." He smiled wryly at Ki. "Somehow, it 'pears you pulled Ev Moran's teeth. That ain't exactly what I'd recommend for good openers."

45

Ki cast him a jaundiced look. "He gave me no choice. What should I've done, drowned the man in oil while I was at it?"

Ferguson sobered. "You could've done worse."

Chapter 4

A burgundy afterglow washed the west slopes of the San Juans with color. As the four rode, it faded slowly, leaving a final flame on the high crests. They approached a broad southerly bend in the desert's course. Continuing straight, they ascended the outer bank of the curve and then climbed toward a hogback, coming soon to a thread-thin trail that meandered in their direction.

By now the sunset's last delicate streamers had vanished, replaced by dusk's purple shadows, and there was only a mauve emptiness to be seen around them. By now, however, Jessie had discerned why the desert was a short cut: The ranch lay in line with the main lobe of the kidney-shaped desert, whereas the wagon road went up around to avoid both the desert and the hogback.

They descended the hogback through squat brush yellow with tiny flowers, and they intersected the main road where it angled down toward the ranch. Shortly, the road ended at a tree-shaded yard.

In and around the yard were a normal amount of clutter and equipment; along with a clapboard barn and a smattering of sheds, there were a substantial pole corral holding some horses, and a large pueblo-style house, flat-roofed, with beam ends jutting from its thick adobe walls. A few hands were working on this or that, and one of them hurried over to take their horses as the four dismounted by the gallery that ran the front length of the house.

"I think some freshenin' up is in order," Ferguson said, eyeing his daughter as well as Ki. "Now, we've only one tub—"

"I'm not fit for a tub," Ki interjected. "You'd never get it clean afterward. Is there a place outside I could scrub off?"

Ferguson nodded. "We've got a little pond back in some rocks. Alice, fetch soap for you and Ki and show him where the pond is, while I get Jessie settled in one of the guest rooms."

"I'll dig a clean pair of jeans out of your bag and have it and your other clothes sent over to you," Jessie told Ki, as Ferguson unstrapped the luggage and started for the front door.

Alice and Ki helped the hand lead the horses to the barn, where she located a couple of bars of homemade lye soap. "Follow me," she said, handing him a bar. "The pond's close. Papa built it for a swimming hole, but sometimes it gets used for special cases like yours."

Countering the dark night, a pale half moon illuminated the weedy path that went from the house toward a rocky knoll. Against the knoll was a clump of boulders, out of which came a trickling brook and the sound of splashing water.

"It was dangerous, Ki, what you did. But, oh, it was

exciting! It must always be exciting, you and Jessie traveling about and facing danger. Now what're you going to do? What plans have you made?"

Ki sensed danger then and there. "Nary a one, Alice."

"I have no plans, either—and nowhere to go."

One glance at Alice smiling coquettishly, and Ki decided to leave her remark strictly alone. As they drew nearer the boulders, Ki noticed bluestem grass growing in tufts at their feet, and indication of a spring or a tank. Once within the screening rock, he saw that it encircled a small patch, which had been artificially dammed and allowed to fill up, causing a small waterfall. A few little animals fled when they moved through the grass, but otherwise the area looked deserted. Satisfied, Ki turned to Alice.

"Thanks. I guess this's where I skin off and dive in."

Alice seemed reluctant to go, reiterating with a sigh, "No plans and nowhere. Being stuck here is awfully dull and boring."

"Strange, I haven't found it that way so far."

"You would if you were a girl," she pouted. "My friends are all married with fat babies, but I don't want to be like them, hitched to a local boy who's dull and boring and too poor to take me anywhere."

Ki was getting intrigued, but he was more interested in getting washed. "Surely you can trap something wearing pants," he retorted scoffingly, "who's got enough—but who's not got too much—so he'd be willing to give his freedom to do it for you and—"

An exasperated gasp escaped Alice. She snatched up a chunk of rotten tree limb and hurled it at Ki, cutting his jibing short. Ki ducked, throwing up an arm to deflect the wood, but it caught him across the nape of the neck and shoulders, disintegrating in a mess that showered down and stuck to Ki's sticky back.

"Now look what you did," he accused, swallowing his laughter, and he began undoing his jeans. "Got me grimier than ever. So clear out, Alice. I've got to shuck down and take my bath now."

Alice retreated immediately with no further argument or flirtation. When she was safely out of sight, Ki stripped naked and plunged from the warm night into the cool water. The bar of soap lathered poorly and was coarse and caustic enough to've etched rawhide, and it stirred blood pulsing through his sore body as he harshly scrubbed clean. He was not quite through when he thought he heard something approach, but seeing nothing in any direction, he chalked it up to a small animal nosing about. Then squatting to his neck, he washed his face and hair and was dunking to rinse off when he heard more sounds—and this time there was no mistaking them.

Alice appeared at the boulders, pausing to stand in their shadows, with her arms clasping his clothes. "Jessie gave these to Manuel, who gave them to me," she said, smiling plumply. "It'll be hard to persuade me to give them to an old ogre like you."

Instinctively Ki crouched. "You vixen! If your father knew—"

"Careful! You be nice, or I'll take them back, along with mine." She moved closer, into the moonlight by pond's edge, and dropped her bundle. She was totally bare. "I don't want to get married. I just want excitement. That's the kind I am, excitable."

"You're more'n that," Ki allowed, involuntarily rising to the occasion. Her nude body was smooth and unblemished; her pointed breasts tipped by raspberry-size nipples swayed gracefully as she eased into the water; her pubic curls like a delicate blond froth accentuated rather than obscured the fleshy crevice between her thighs.

She waded closer. "Now that you're clean, I can see that your face is bruised and your eyebrow is cut," she cooed sympathetically and slid the palm of her hand along the rugged plane of his cheeks. "Poor dear. Let me make it better."

She kissed him, her hand sidling down between them toward his hardening erection. Even while calling himself a sucker, Ki found himself kissing Alice back. She made a whimpering sound in her throat, still not breaking the kiss as she traced the thickening column of his aroused manhood.

"Cut it out," he protested huskily. "They'll be waiting for us. Your father'll worry, come looking. If we got caught by him—"

"Or Jessie?" Alice teased, silencing Ki with a finger to his mouth. "Then don't make me raise a loud stink, like I do when I don't get my way. Papa would bullwhip us both. But that's the lovely danger of it, why it's so exciting. Oh, kiss my breasts, kiss 'em!"

This is crazy, Ki thought. Hers was a blatant challenge, was a passion deluxe, and what man could resist that? He kissed her lips, her cheeks, the tender hollow of her neck; then he bent lower to lave and suckle her hardened nipples. She moaned, her flesh melting to his liquid caresses, and her voice sighed in his ear, begging him to possess her completely and quench the perverse fires in her belly.

"Be fast, be fast," she pleaded, straddling him there in the water. "Ahh, but how I'd love to have it last longer than it can!"

Ki pressed slowly, gently, and felt her stretching to accept him. He slid deeply up inside her, against increasing internal resistance. Her slim body trembled. She

51

breathed raggedly through her mouth. "More, more . . . All of you . . . Don't stop, yes . . ."

Glancing down at their merging loins in the dim pond, Ki was surprised that she was managing to absorb him to the hilt. She was so petite and nubile, yet she was enveloping his entire length and girth. Her eyes fluttered as his pelvis nudged against her mound, and she mewed soulfully as he withdrew slightly, his shaft moist with her secretions. Then he pumped back up into her, again and again, his tempo quickening while he embraced her supportively, and his mouth once again closed around her throbbing breasts.

Alice shuddered and gasped, whining, her words unintelligible but their meaning clear. She was urging him on, moving her hips in concert and helping to piston with increasing rapidity, breathless for her oncoming release. He drove furiously into her, while she lowered her head, kissing his neck and nibbling his ears. All of a sudden he levered upward, freezing into quivering rigidity and erupting into orgasm, spilling hot and boiling into her depths as she twisted against him spasmodically with her own spiraling climax. He deflated quickly, but she didn't move from astride him right away, continuing to hold him gently inside her.

She kissed him again. "Nice?"

"Damn nice," he murmured against her hair.

"Let's be nice again later." She smiled kittenishly as she eased off him, and they started for the grassy edge of the pond. "My, it certainly is later," she remarked, a twinge of self-consciousness stealing over her as she walked for the boulders. "We better hurry, Ki. Pardon me while I go get dressed."

Ki found that a towel had been included with his clothes, and after drying himself hastily, he put on his clean duds and waited for Alice. There was soreness all over his body, and strangely, he felt more invigorated after his erotic workout than before.

Alice came back wearing a tweed skirt and a frilly blouse, looking fresh and demure as if the whole affair had been a figment of Ki's imagination. She scanned his bruised face again and clucked her tongue. "That must've been a dilly of a fight. Moran's bad, Ki, bad pure through. High, low, or foul, he'll try to pay you back."

"Yeah, he didn't act like one who'd likely forget."

"Watch yourself." She stretched to give Ki a peck on the cheek, then turned and headed ranchward on the path. Ki fell to following her, more than satisfied to let her blaze the way. She did.

Ferguson was pacing the gallery when they arrived. "I'd about given up on you! What held you up so long, Ki?" he demanded.

"My thoughts precisely," Alice said before Ki could answer. "So I went and called to him, and darn near woke him up," she lied blithely. "I'm famished. Let's go in and put on the feedbag."

Mollified, Ferguson led them inside, oblivious to the fact that they brought back two damp towels, not just one. Ki didn't point this out, either, but discreetly discarded the towels with his oil-ruined jeans in his guest room, preferring to keep silent and take the blame for having dozed in the pond.

When he returned, he found everyone including Jessie seated at the dining room table. He took his place, and a moment later the fat, middle-aged housekeeper and cook, named Bertha, rolled in a serving tray laden with food. The meal proved to be a belly-burster, starting with a tureen of raisins and rice, moving on through beets, chuck roast, and boiled cabbage, and winding down with pumpkin pie and coffee, with all the trimmings between. It also proved to be a leisurely one, conversation lively and often amusing as old times were recounted and new times were discussed.

"We've got a war in the brewin'," Ferguson was saying a long time afterward, as they sat around the table with no thought yet of going to bed. "Another to-the-last-man feudin'. We've got to nip it in the bud, fast."

"What steps have you taken so far?" Jessie asked.

"Well, I've posted guards along with the reg'lar linemen, but we really don't have enough hands to patrol effectively. We don't hit town alone, not after our man Lusk got shot by Moran, and we run our riders in pairs when they're on Cartinas's side of the slopes. If you mean retaliation, though, I haven't considered it in any form."

"That's sensible," she agreed. "Two wrongs never make a right."

"But there's a limit to patience," Ferguson went on gravely. "Me and my men are becomin' increasingly irritated, what with Lusk bein' shot and others bein' shot at, and the rustling and poisoning."

"Not particularly unnatural," Ki admitted with a grin and paused while the grandfather clock in the hall chimed eleven o'clock before continuing, "Getting riled at folks isn't the same as getting proof against them. That's what we need, solid facts, more and better than the footprints you found going south from the poisoned spring."

"I just made them up, to get Moran's goat," Ferguson confessed, and he met Jessie's quizzical glance. "Frankly, Ramon and Ysabelle Cartinas don't strike me as the sort who'd poison cattle to even a score. I'd expect their methods to be more direct. I wasn't fibbing about their crew, though. They're plenty on the prod, like ours, and maybe some of 'em cut loose to do it on their own."

"Maybe," Jessie allowed, "but from what I saw of the *señora*, I seriously doubt she or her husband would let their men get out of control, any more than you would allow yours here to. Do you know of anyone else hereabouts who could profit from a row like this?"

Ferguson shook his head. "No. Of course, there's any number of owlhoots maverickin' around right now, attracted by the oil strike, and p'raps they'd figure to cash in on a big feud somehow. One thing I'm not guessing about: It won't be a picnic, if it does come. Cartinas didn't build his spread by wearing mittens. He's got a packed bunkhouse, and just he and his wife alone have got more hell in them than all their ancestors rolled together."

Jessie frowned. She did not minimize the gravity of the situation and the ominous possibilities it held. The smell of gun powder was in the air. Ki too was aware of it, but he was also aware of a woman with raven-black hair and a spirit as wild as these untamed hills, in which she had been born.

Their thoughts were abruptly ended by a pounding on the front door. Bertha hurried to answer, and a squabbling of voices erupted in the hall, followed by the appearance of four ranch hands at the dining room entry. Two of them were supporting the third man, who was groggily conscious and looking as if he'd suffered a terrible beating. The fourth man, ignoring Bertha's nagging protests, stalked toward the startled group at the table.

"Boss, we found Vince like this, battered to a pulp and roped unconscious to his horse," the fourth man announced.

"Che-rist!" Ferguson blurted, coming out of his chair. So did the others, grouping around the injured man as

55

he was gently settled on a settee. He motioned that it would take a moment for him to recover his breath and speak; Ferguson spent the moment acknowledging the hands and introducing them to Jessie and Ki.

Like Vince, the two who'd helped him were regular punchers. The fourth man proved to be the foreman, Hugh Picket—called "High-pocket"—who was a lean, bow-legged veteran of the range and seemed to be put together of leather and steel braid.

Through a swollen mouth of loose teeth, Vince began to talk, "Me and Syracuse hadn't a chance," he whispered, grimacing with pain. "We was circlin' back on our tour o' the east slopes and was jumped this side o' the ford. Y'know the one, near the Cartinas line in the bottoms. They knocked me outta the saddle and was all over me afore I knew. I made a grab for 'em and got one afore I was clubbed under and kicked cold."

"When Vince grabbed, he netted this," High-pocket said and handed Ferguson a broken length of heavy gold chain. Ferguson regarded it and gave it to Jessie, who thought it resembled the sort of pocket watch chain that a man used when wearing a vest. High-pocket added, "Vince still had it in his fist when we found him."

"Did you see who these men were?" Ki asked Vince.

Vince weakly shook his head. "Too dark. Moon hadn't come up yet. And it happened too swift for me to catch faces. Five or six of 'em, I think, but I couldn't recognize any of 'em if I saw 'em right now."

"Uh-huh. Well, what about Syracuse? Where's he?"

"Outside. Dead. We found him with his head bashed in." High-pocket cast a proud glance at Vince. "Vince wouldn't let us carry him in, not till we backtrailed to check out what happened."

"So it's come to killin', has it," Ferguson growled,

nodding with a sort of grim miserableness. "And the bunch they were tendin'?"

"It was culled, Boss. The unborn stuff is still there, out on the southeast bench, but upwards of eighty head, trailing calf, are gone. And every one of them spindle-legs unbranded as yet." High-pocket's weathered face screwed into an outraged scowl. "How is Starbuck set for a fight against steep-stacked odds? How much prodding does it take? And the boys have got to know this: Does Starbuck raise the ante when powder-smoke goes with their beans?"

Jessie answered, since she was *the* Starbuck. "I pay any wage that's earned," she snapped, her eyes measuring High-pocket and the two able hands with him. She knew well enough that it wasn't promise of fighting pay that would hold these and the other crewmen; she knew that her own reaction to this news, her own first steps, would serve as an indication to them of what to expect when a Starbuck ranch was being pressured. Whatever else was coming they would judge by her—even Ferguson would do this—and whether or not the ranch would retain a crew with which to work depended on these brief moments. She added, "So our stock's been rustled. Then where did they go?"

"I know which way they were being driven, but not where they finally went. And for good reason." High-pocket pulled off his hat and ran his fingers through a pair of holes in its crown, front to back. "We tracked the drive to Cartinas's boundary, south of our bottom sections. Cartinas had men on their line, and one of them was mighty handy with a rifle. What with Vince in bad shape, 'n all, I figured we'd better skin for here before we got reckless."

Jessie, pursing her lips, remembered the hard animosity of Ysabelle Cartinas and Ev Moran and their grim intention to bull through on a set course of action against any odds. Cartinas was suffering from severe stock losses and lack of operating cash and was gathering a herd to sell off quickly to the railroad. Matured cattle, running under another brand, could be burned over and passed as one's own, but unbranded calves were an even easier way to increase a herd, being impossible to challenge once they'd been iron-marked. To Jessie, the thought that while she'd been taling to Ysabelle and Moran, other Cartinas riders had been preparing to put burrs under her saddle, stung deeply. It was raw work, needing a raw response.

High-pocket, watching her face, began to grin for the first time. "Wild country, south of that line, and broken to all heck, but with plenty of cover. I've scouted down that way upon occasion."

"Agin my orders!" Ferguson barked.

"Gosh, I must've had a spell or two of forgetfulness." High-pocket grinned wider. "It's okay; I wasn't spotted. And I reckon we could cut east 'round that line and come in that way again, without maybe being pot-shot at by some son with a sharp-sighted rifle."

Jessie asked, "How many of the crew'll side such a ride?"

"All," High-pocket declared, the two hands nodding agreement.

"We'd sound like an army," Ferguson objected, mulling this over. "Getting everybody would take too long anyway, and it'd leave the spread wide empty. Besides, things gotta look normal here, so we don't let out what's coming. Now, y'all and me makes four—"

"Six, including us," Jessie corrected.

"Hold on! Ki can go, if he's hankerin', but you're a lady!"

"I'm the owner, Ian. I go or nobody goes."

"She's also a crack shot and steady under fire," Alice chimed in. "I can vouch for that. But please, Papa, wait! You heard their threats. If you go busting over there, there'll be blood spilled."

Ferguson regarded his daughter, his features almost truculent. "Sure, and most of it'll be Cartinas blood. Don't get no notions either, gal. You ain't no owner pullin' rank. You're staying here and helpin' Bertha nurse Vincent." He sighed then, the sigh of a man plagued by women. "Okay, six of us. Sounds about a right number."

"And the Cartinas tally?" Ki asked.

"Near twenty," High-pocket replied. "They don't rattle."

Ferguson rubbed his hands together. "Neither do we."

Chapter 5

In another fifteen minutes the six were tracking out of the ranch yard. Souteastward they swept, their horses's irons ringing across the rock-studded rangeland. Ahead and on their right below were the bottom sections, pale and silver in the moonlight. Behind and on their left above was the dark gloom of the immediate hills, rolling upward till their jagged crests stood out against the misty sky. And beyond lurked Cartinas's spread, shrouded in black mystery.

Mile after mile flowed under the speeding hooves of the horses. Jessie and Ki were mostly silent, and Ferguson grumbled profanely now and then. Occasionally talk drifted from High-pocket and the two hands; their talk was not loud, but there was a repressed eagerness, which Jessie and Ki found wholly lacking in themselves. They had seen men spill blood and had spilled a bit of it themselves. They had seen some good come of grim riding such as this, but had seen a great deal of evil sprout from the same well-intentioned roots.

At length they reached the floor of the bottoms, with the much lower trough of the desert due west, and the plateau of hills surrounding them on the other three sides. The natural wash of the eroding slopes and underground water-table had formed a more fertile base here, nurturing thickets of bindweed and thorny brush.

"The bottoms end soon, now, and then we'll be on Cartinas's land," Ferguson said. "High-pocket, 'fess up. You sure you know the track?"

His foreman grunted assent. "Even if I didn't, I'd still go looking for it. High time someone stuck a bee in Cartinas's ear. They've been lording this region since I can recollect, and it's been a long wait for 'em to get their fingers caught in the cookie jar."

"You figure they have?" Jessie asked.

"If not Cartinas, Miss Starbuck, who else?"

Jessie shook her head, but made no further comment. Instead she sorted her knowledge of the Cartinas legend, the big Spanish-granted ranch, and the woman who helped her husband run it. There had been lawlessness among early members of that savage clan, and it had been these who had built much of the legend. And lawlessness could run in the blood of a family. Coupled to this was the strong impression that Ysabelle Cartinas had a fanatic passion for her land—that she would do anything to preserve it, including vying with her hated neighbors. These things boiled down into the elements of a maverick outfit, rodded by Ev Moran and staffed by a loyal, tough crew.

Yet no clear proof existed that the cattle had been stolen by Cartinas. The only solid facts were that they'd been driven onto Cartinas's land, and that the Cartinas boundary had subsequently been defended. And regardless of the justness of this foray, when men rode ready to deal death, death seldom avoided their readiness.

Jessie rode for one paramount reason. Trouble lay dark over her ranch. Alone, faced with the necessity of keeping it rolling, she'd be helpless. She had to have the nucleus of a crew. And she had headed other operations too long not to know that if she'd refused to act now, High-pocket, the hands, and probably Ferguson, too, would figure her a weakling and quit her cold. Or equally bad, they would elect to strike out on their own. She wanted her cattle back. She wanted to answer Cartinas, if this was a Cartinas move. But mostly she wanted to lead these men judiciously now, to protect them from reckless bloodshed, and retain them for greater need later.

High-pocket forged a circuitous, cautious trail, but he seemed to know it well. They forded a dry stream bed, then forded it twice again in the next half hour, weaving east along the bottoms at a fast pace. Far behind them, the faint outlines of the oil derricks faded from view, leaving only the creak of saddle leather, the jingle of iron bits, and the shuffling whisper of trodden earth and brush to break the oppressive loneliness encompassing them.

Shortly they quit the stream bed and ascended, their course bending constantly so that it changed from east to just south of east and then to full south. They were undeniably trespassing now, climbing through Cartinas hills. They were, on average, lower and gentler of grade and crest, and had denser growth than the stark, sheer slopes that flanked the desert and bottoms on the north.

They were deep up in these hills when High-pocket dropped them into a narrow valley and aimed them straight into the heart of Cartinas's vast range. When they emerged onto a high bench, lush with graze, he rode more slowly.

After a lengthy stretch of cutting to and fro across open country, he reined in and scratched his head.

"It don't make sense," he said uneasily. "Nobody'd be fool enough to hold hot stuff any lower than this. But there's only two ways stock could be driven up here, and we've cut across both those draws and there's no sign of a recent drive. I'm stumped."

"Y'mean our cows ain't been led up here?" Ferguson demanded. "That's same as saying they ain't on Cartinas land at all."

"Yeah, Boss, else they *would* be here. And at the same time, I saw the drive-track head straight across Cartinas's line, and these holes in my hat tell me I wasn't seeing crooked."

"Night is a poor time to unravel anything, High-pocket," Jessie consoled. "I agree with you, but for a different reason. If Cartinas was holding our cattle anywhere near, he'd have guards out and we'd have cut ourselves into a slice of trouble already."

Ferguson nodded. "Sure. Best is to backtrack and shake out a new loop tomorrow. Maybe tomorrow we'll have some better luck."

Reluctantly High-pocket acquiesced. "Okay, but let's grab a shortcut to the bottoms," he suggested. "We'll save a mile or so."

They started their return, descending through draws and along banked pastures, sometimes blazing their own path, sometimes using a trail if it angled their way. Taking a more direct route increased the risk of detection, and their man worry was that a Cartinas rider might chance by and hear the click of their horses's shoes on the stones. They searched the dark loom of the slopes and surrounding underbrush, but all was silent and deserted—

Until Jessie exclaimed, "Don't I hear horses?"

63

Ki listened intently. "You hear more than a horse," he said. "You hear cows, a lot of them, and horses with them, heading at us."

Jessie sensed, rather than saw, Ferguson reach for his revolver. Instantly she leaned across and clamped a hand around his wrist.

"Lemme go," he whispered fiercely. "Those're your cows!"

"Whoever they are, if we go charging them, they're apt to trample right over us, if the riders don't shoot us first," she argued and then glanced about. Not far from them was a belt of thicket. "Into that brush there till we can check what we're up against."

They veered off the trail and filed into the growth, dismounting where they could view the trail without being spotted. Ferguson, muttering under his breath, slid his carbine out of his saddle boot and levered a shell into its chamber. The others followed suit with their rifles and sidearms. Ki had accepted the loan of a Winchester just in case the need arose, like now, for long-range weaponry. Then taking up positions where outcrops of stone afforded additional cover, they waited tensely, watching the trail and hearing the drum of hooves and bawl of cows grow louder and louder.

Suddenly a massive shadow bulged around a bend in the trail. It swiftly developed into a herd of cattle approaching at a rapid clip. Short, querulous bleats burst from the sweating cows, their labored breath whistling through flaring nostrils as they were shoved along close-bunched by expert point, flank, and drag riders.

Jessie and Ki exchanged glances with the same grim thought. No legitimate crew would be running the fat of stock like this, and the herd, they judged, fairly well matched in number the estimate High-pocket had given of stolen cattle. These were Starbuck cattle.

Yet Jessie wished to avoid bloodshed. "Don't forget we're on Cartinas's land," she called. "Shoot to miss; shoot to chase them away. If we happen to wing a couple, we'll be all right, but we wouldn't have a chance of bulling through if this turned into a killing spree."

"Damn Cartinas!" Ferguson swore. "I'll aim to scare, but if they come after us, we'll hafta take the steam outta 'em but fast."

The jostling, jumbled herd thundered in and on by, along with the point and a few flanking riders. Following came the majority of riders, grouped behind on the narrow trail. Jessie shouldered her carbine and sighted on a target . . . But it was High-pocket who impatiently triggered the first shot, and that shot acted as a signal.

A rattling barrage erupted from the thicket. Only one rider reeled clinging to his saddle horn, apparently clipped by too close a bullet. The rest of those riding drag wheeled, alarmed, and fell awry, disorganized yet far from routed. Nor did the point and flank riders panic, but galloped back to join in. The rustler crew hastily recovered and brought their own weapons into play.

Jessie ducked to reload, as the riders swerved in at an angle to the thicket, charging disorderly while firing volleys of lead. It was now kill or be killed, and Jessie cursed the sullen stubbornness of Cartinas, the contrariness of Cartinas blood.

She and the other five returned fire, this time for keeps. Theirs was good, steady shooting, despite the wan moonlight and the confusion of cows. The throaty blasts of repeaters, the sharper crack of revolvers, the pounding hooves and howling oaths as the riders converged on the thicket . . . it was a deafening, roiling storm, all but ignored as bodies were tracked and death meted out.

Jessie fired, levered, and fired more, ignoring the ache in her shoulder from the recoil of her borrowed carbine. She caught one rider, who toppled against another, both of them falling to the ground. The second man rolled and scrambled into a run, only to be downed when Ferguson's round struck him in the chest. Ferguson let out a bull-voiced hurraw and speedily emptied a third saddle. High-pocket and two hands were slamming out shots as fast as they could, while Ki was triggering with rhythmic care, blowing a fourth and then a fifth rider out of their hulls.

Bellows of shock and pain rent the air, the withering defense from the thicket halting the onrush of the riders, whose force was now cut by fully a third. Those remaining turned aside, circling and breaking, and then began to retreat behind a covering fusillade. Ki felt the wind of a passing bullet. Another tugged the sleeve of Jessie's denim jacket. High-pocket roared blasphemously, as a third slug drilled yet another hole through his hat.

With a last few random shots, the riders scattered, vanishing in the direction they had come from. This perplexed Jessie, as she rose from concealment. From what she'd gathered, heading down toward the bottom would not be the most direct route to the Cartinas stronghold. Nor could she understand why, inasmuch as tonight's rustling jig was finished, there would be any further need for roundabout maneuvers.

Yet this was a minor puzzle, which she promptly dismissed as she met with the others gathered around one of the hands. He lay prostrate, flinching and gritting his teeth while Ferguson, hunkering alongside, prodded and poked inside his bloody shirt. Ferguson straightened in

66

a moment, the man looking up appealingly for his verdict.

"You got a hefty gouge along your ribs, best I can tell," Ferguson said, "the sort that smarts worse'n it really is. We'll bind you up and have you at the ranch in a jiffy, Ralph. You'll mend fine."

"Let me," High-pocket offered, removing his shirt to rip it into bandages. "Stand aside, y'all, and let the doctor operate."

Jessie said to Ki, "While he's doing that, I want to look over the men we downed there in the trail. Wish their horses hadn't hightailed after the others, so I could've checked their brands."

Ki nodded. Ferguson, overhearing her, joined them and said, "They're Cartinas mounts; they hafta be. Careful now, if one of those galoots is playing possum, we could get shot afore knowin' it."

However, the five riders were thoroughly dead. They were ornery looking cusses, but with nothing outstanding about them, and they wore typical rangeland garb—worn overalls, scruffy chaps, and sun-faded shirts. Their pockets contained only insignificant belongings, but the seams of their linings appeared to interest Ki, so much so that he ripped one pocket loose and stowed it away.

"Souvenir," he remarked casually. "Well, it looks like Ralph is all wrapped up tidy, so let's get those cows turned for home. They're so tired they didn't stampede, despite the racket."

"Amen to that," Ferguson declared fervently. "The sooner we get out of here, the better we'll be."

"Too late for that," a gruff voice called acidly, "but at least you're smart, Ferguson, and already said your prayers."

Pivoting, they saw the trail was blocked at both ends. Ev Moran sat asaddle a few yards uptrail, two other horsemen appearing behind him from brush along the far side, while three more emerged at a similar distance downtrail. Each was training a revolver.

These six couldn't have just ridden up, Ki realized, else they'd have been heard. No, they must've sneaked in and postioned themselves during the battle, then waited for their opportunity. It was a pretty neat trap, which was sprung when he, Jessie, and Ferguson mistakenly gathered, exposed and vulnerable, on the open trail.

"Get your pals out here," Moran ordered, as he and his men closed in. "Anyone tries a trick, and you're all gone ducks."

High-pocket and the hands, including the wounded Ralph, stepped clear of the thicket of their own volition. At the same time, Ki began walking casually toward Moran, no expression on his face. But he recalled Moran beaten and bloody and threatening revenge.

"I guessed twenty to the Cartinas crew," High-pocket growled sourly. "I wasn't off more'n one or two. Fat good that."

By then Ki had strolled up to Moran and read his bottled savagery, the neurotic pleasure for brutality, inherent in the man's features. Calmly he said, "There's no more need for gunplay."

"Yeah? Seems you can't take a hint."

Ferguson snapped, "Taking our cows comes before minding hints."

Moran shifted in his seat, and moonlight glinted dully off the barrel of his Colt. "But why are you taking them up here?"

"You're crazy! We—"

"Shut up!" Moran commanded, his thumb clicking

back the hammer. "We caught you dead to rights—and dead is the big word."

Ki poised to move, but hadn't yet when another rider broke out onto the trail. "Ev—!" a woman's voice cried warningly.

Ysabelle Cartinas spurred forward. It was plain that however wild the Cartinas crew might be, she had control of it, for all the horsemen gave her a swift and ready sort of deference.

Probably Moran would have as well, but he was too absorbed in firing to notice anything else. He was tipping his revolver at Ki, his long finger squeezing the trigger. Ki lashed out and grabbed his wrist, deflecting his aim, and the .45 slug blasted a shade over Ki's head. By then he had his other hand clutching Moran by the near ankle. Wrenching hard, he yanked Moran from the saddle.

Moran dropped heavily to the trail, cursing, his revolver landing a couple of feet away. He immediately scrambled up and was lunging for his revolver when Ki kicked him square in the face with his right foot. Moran screamed as his nose shattered from the impact. He was almost lifted from the ground and fell over on his left side, blood spurting from his crunched nose and upper lip.

While the horsemen chafed angrily, stymied by the presence of their boss, Ki punted Moran's revolver off into the thicket and went over to Ysabelle. "Your massacre is cancelled for tonight," he said stonily. "Your rustling didn't completely work as planned, either."

"Massacre?" Ysabelle repeated quizzically, staring at Ki with eyes as friendless as Moran's had been. "Rustling? *Zoquete*—lying dog!"

Jessie, moving up beside Ki, responded tensely, "We were drawn and now snared on your property, our herd cut, one crewman dead, and two injured. That's most of what you're after, isn't it?"

Ysabelle turned on Jessie. "Your cows, your crew! What do I care about them? Nothing! Nothing, so long as you stay away."

"No?" Jessie was unconvinced. "Then what was intended? Why were cattle driven here, and why were we suckered into this trap?"

Ysabelle didn't answer at once, but looked at Moran on the ground. He had risen to his heels and was swabbing the ruin of his face, glancing malevolently at Ki. Ysabelle's eyes raised. She studied Jessie, and again Jessie felt the hard power within her.

"Do you believe we're so easily tricked? That my men fail to ride our line, and one wouldn't soon find signs of the drive? Or that later, when more raiders tried to follow it across, they'd be stopped by rifles, no questions asked? Or that we wouldn't want to track that drive? True, we lost it on the slabstone flats, but considering it was a night-drive traveling fast, there was only one place it could have gone—up into our breaks, to be left for stolen evidence. So we scoured our hills, heard the gunfire, and came. But you think us so foolish that we'd rush headlong into bullets?" Ysabelle paused, compressing her lips, then added, "We are the trapped, and you the trappers. If you weren't planting stock on us, then why are you here, miles deep inside Cartinas range?"

Jessie replied quietly, "Trying to find nearly a hundred head of our cattle, many of them unmarked as yet, that were driven over here."

"So you were rustled, and we're to get blamed," Ysabelle said with irony. "It fits; it explains much." Her voice harshened. "But it doesn't excuse your invasion, your fighting on my land."

70

"A chunk of my herds had been run onto your land. What should we've done, come discuss it like neighbors?" Jessie retorted. "No, not with Señora Cartinas. We had our chat about that earlier. Well, I'd still like for us to talk, and I've got something to return."

"Talk? Talk doesn't pay bills or taxes, or grow grass or work cattle. Talk doesn't help me run my ranch by myself, alone, when half the state is pitched against it because of how the Cartinas grandfather and great-grandfather were. I've had enough of talk."

Jessie saw a great deal about Ysabelle in this moment. There was no outward sign, but she saw that the woman was desperate, and that the obstinate pride which upheld her was cracking. She saw that the ranch was more than a home; it was a weary burden and a ruthless challenge which Ysabelle would not or could not refuse.

"It would be too much alone, talk or no talk," she replied softly, feeling a quick wave of sympathy. "But with your husband—"

"So you wish to talk to Ramon, too!" Ysabelle laughed bitterly. "You are new, Señorita Starbuck, and I don't yet know which way your shadow lies. But come along, and maybe I'll cure you of talk."

"Now?"

"*Como no!*—why not?"

"Jessie, no!" Ferguson called aghast. "Not alone!"

"With Ki," Jessie responded, intrigued by Ysabelle's cryptic invitation. "If we're not in by noon, you can send a wagon for us."

Ferguson threw up his hands. "Good luck," he said gruffly. "I reckon the three an' a half of us can get these pooped cows home."

"My boys'll help," Moran proposed, which raised hackles on both crews. He had risen, was dusting himself

71

off, and eyed his riders and then Ferguson's men with a scowl that brooked no argument. "I don't want no mix-ups, is why," he added truculently, swinging to his saddle. "I don't want none of our stuff wanderin' over there, and none of their stuff left remainin' over here."

"Not a bad idea," High-pocket allowed, "but not a choice to everyone's taste, as the herder said when he kissed his sheep."

Jessie and Ki fetched their horses and, while Ferguson stared beleagueredly after them, departed overland with Ysabelle and Moran. Plunging down the hills, they passed through a series of valleys and scrub meadows whose graze was not prime, Jessie noticed, but looked better than what little she'd seen of hers to the north. Yet it all appeared to lie fallow, unstocked, nary a cow in sight.

"We've collected many small bunches into a close herd near the San Joaquin hills," Ysabelle replied to a question. "Soon as we finish rooting strays out of the broken sections and canyons, we'll push to San Clemente. The hills are bad, rough country, wicked to drive across, and one reason I don't mind the railroad up here. But if it's coming because of the oil that's spoiling the water and grass and killing off stock, then it will do me more harm than good."

Shortly they began crossing a section of range where the grass looked sere, with patches of soil showing between the tufts. "You ain't squinted at nothin' yet," Moran growled when Ki remarked at the difference. After another quarter of a mile or so, they reached a shallow, slow-flowing stream. Nearby and along its banks, the ground-cover was but crisped straggle, utterly dead and drying up.

"See what I mean?" Ysabelle asked. "Oil all over it."

The summer-becalmed stream had a peculiar appearance, its trickling surface reflecting the moonlight in a dusty rainbow sheen that was singularly smooth and glassy. Both Jessie and Ki frowned as they gazed curiously at the iridescent water, knowing the cause, yet...

"Does this creek run near the desert?" Jessie asked.

Ysabelle shook her head. "Not very. It comes from a canyon in the hills and dives in and out of the ground like so many streams in these parts. None of them gets very close to the desert, but the wells spill oil over everything, and there is a back-flow under pressure from the big reserves beneath the desert, so I'm told, that causes oil to seep up through the grass and into the water."

"And you say your stock's died from it?" Jessie persisted.

"Si, we find them stretched out stiff not far from one of these stinking spots, so poisoned even the buzzards won't peck at them."

"Funny. I've rarely heard of a vulture turning down a meal." Thoughtfully Jessie stared in the direction of the desert. Something seemed to be baffling her, but she didn't question further.

They rode on. Ki, his memory jogged by Jessie's puzzled expression, took out the pocket he had torn from the dead man's overalls and passed it across to Jessie. "Look at the lining."

Examining it, Jessie found the seams were caked with a greasy grit that washing had been unable to remove. Nodding, she handed back the pocket. "I see. That rider must've hung around the wells."

"Oil men!" Ysabelle spat. "Is there no end to their evil?"

"Those rustlers were good at stock handling," Jessie replied, "and they certainly didn't ride or dress like most oil workers."

"Oh, I don't mean the ones who drill the holes and put up the towers and so forth," Ysabelle hastened to explain. "I mean the big hombres who the oil men hire by the dozen for cheap labor."

"Yeah, a menial job at the wells would cover any gent wanting to stay here unnoticed," Ki agreed and stowed the pocket away. "Question is, where are they holed up?"

For the present, his was a question without hope of answer. The conversation limped along, Jessie and Ki giving up any effort to encourage it. Ysabelle and Moran seemed wrapped in some deep brooding, but their eyes were active, never ceasing their alert sweep of the way ahead and the surrounding terrain.

It put a creepy feeling into a person, and Jessie was glad when into view came an acreage of sheds, corrals, bunkhouses, and finally the great residence itself.

If a house could resemble its builders, then Cartinas's place resembled the Cartinas clan. Set advantageously by a grove of ancient burr oaks, it was a thick 'dobe that looked capable of withstanding a seige and sprawled in the rectangular shape which made for functional living in this arid country. Solid and aged, it was indelibly part and parcel of the history of California.

They angled to avoid the corrals and work buildings and drove straight to the wide fronting veranda of the house. Light shone from the big salon within, illuminating the yard for them as they reined in and dismounted—though by now the moon was fading, and the gray blear of false dawn was beginning to soften the sky.

"So you wish to meet Ramon. *Muy bien,* come in and see what the last of the Cartinas men has met already. Come in and see why Cartinas's fight is mine and mine alone, and why I'll stick as long as there's hoof or hide of Cartinas stock on these hills!"

Ysabelle stalked into the house. Jessie and Ki hesitated to follow her and slowed when they climbed to the veranda.

Ev Moran spoke from the lower step. "Go ahead," he growled. "You asked for this. But keep your jaws shut. If either of you says one word, one thing to hurt that lady—"

The foreman's pause was significant. Jessie and Ki crossed the veranda and entered the house. Inside was cool and, save for the salon, dimly lit. The house was filled with heavy, shadowy furniture and an air of rich, quiet comfort. Ysabelle went through the salon, traversed a short hall, and flung open a door. It led into an airy south room, set with many windows and doors to an inner patio.

A bedlike couch was in the center of the room. A man lay on it, fully clothed, but obviously helpless. He appeared to be in his late sixties, his lined face sagging from a spiritual as well as physical weariness, his black eyes tired and vague, almost vacant. There was no movement about his body except for the eyes, which wandered to Ysabelle as she ushered Jessie and Ki toward him. Jessie recognized the brand of the Cartinas blood. The invalid had apparently been a big man, hard and crusty in his prime, and even now, though terribly gaunt, he still exhibited an square iron jaw and the unruly black hair of his kind.

"Ramon, these are our neighbors," Ysabelle said quietly. "Crowding us, like the rest." She turned from her husband. "Ramon Cartinas, the fourth and the last— Señorita Starbuck," she said.

Shocked by the distressing sight, Jessie made a move with Ki to leave. "I . . . I'm sorry to've disturbed you, Señor Cartinas."

"No peace in my home," Ramon complained in a whispered croak, but whether it was a reply to Jessie was unclear. "Never any peace. Home of my father and his father before him, he who rode with the great Coronado, and was awarded his grant by the Spanish king..."

"Rest, Ramon. Your title is secure, verified in court."

Ramon drifted into a fog. "I said go away, leave us alone—when he insisted I sell land to him to ruin..."

Jessie glanced at Ysabelle. "Who?"

Ysabelle gave a cold smile. "One of the new oil men."

"I sent him away with a flea in his ear, *no es verdad?*" Ramon trailed off mumbling querulously in Spanish. *"Es una cara dura..."*

"Hush, now." Ysabelle leaned over her husband for a moment, brushing his forehead with her hand and soothing him silent, then led the way back out into the hall. When she had closed the door to the room, she leaned against it.

"Paralyzed and disoriented," she said impersonally. "A nerve pressure caused by injury to the spine. And if you think death is terrible, then you don't know what it means to him lying there, day and night, dressed and undressed and fed like a baby. None of his family—my family now by marriage—was born to die flat on his back!"

"An injury—" Ki murmured.

"Si, an injury," Ysabelle snapped, "from the bullet of an unknown cowardly assassin." She was moving through the house toward the front door again. "Satisfied? You've heard talk of the Cartinases and wanted to see them up close. Now you have, like hunters after game, looking up at a wounded bear that's got a bullet from every gun in the party in him."

Jessie shook her head as they followed Ysabelle onto

the veranda. "We came this day for the same reason we came on your land initially. There was trouble tonight, more trouble before that, and the only way to stop trouble is to learn the facts, to flush it out with the truth."

"All you've done is bring trouble," Ysabelle scoffed. "And something else, didn't you say? Something you brought to return?"

"If it belongs to anyone here, yes." Jessie glanced at Moran, who'd been waiting by the bottom step, then back at Ysabelle, and plumbed her pocket for the broken watch chain. "The rustlers waylaid two of our hands, killed one, and left the other roughed up badly with this in his fist." She draped the chain across the veranda rail.

Moran stared at the chain with a stony face. "Don't nobody call me a liar when I'm through talking," he said slowly, "because that's one thing I won't swallow. I lost that chain, watch and all, somewhere half a dozen miles from your spread, more'n a week ago. It's mine, okay. But I haven't been across our line since me'n Señora Cartinas got back here from our fandango with you at the oil field."

Jessie studied Moran. In spite of Ysabelle lending silent substantiation to the foreman's story, she was not entirely convinced. But what she and Ki had seen and heard here had set a new course of thought at work in her mind. She smiled faintly.

"Moran, we're caught in crosscurrents I haven't had time to measure. But I'll make a deal. I like to have neighbors and friends, but I've no interest in the Cartinases one way or another. Accept my word for that, and I'll accept your word about the watch."

Moran slanted a look up at Ysabelle. She stated flatly, "A curious neighbor is the last person I'd trust. You have heard of what we have been and, *muy bien,* you've seen what we are—now get out. And remember this: Cartinas is hurt, but he is not dead."

Jessie and Ki remounted and turned thoughtfully toward the Starbuck-owned ranch. Either Ysabelle was a cool, ruthless liar or the whole situation was altogether different from what either of them had supposed it to be; that much was evident. Nothing else was.

Chapter 6

Refreshed after sleeping through most of the morning, Jessie and Ki joined the Fergusons in the dining room for a late brunch.

Alice was in chirpy good humor, evidently enjoying her duty as nurse to Vincent, the hand still weak but showing signs of steady improvement. Her father had a haggard look about him, like a man who hadn't had much rest. Indeed he hadn't; driving the weary and disgusted herd took lengthy effort, especially after Cartinas's riders had quit helping at the boundary line.

The prodigious task made Jessie realize and respect the sort of top manager Ferguson was. It confirmed her opinion of him as an intelligent, diligent man who was deeply concerned with the welfare of the ranch, as well as of the area in general . . . and it added to her budding sense of personal attraction, a tentative awareness that bordered on sexual arousal. Not that she had any such designs in mind, she hastily thought; it was one thing to admire the man and quite another to desire him.

"I want to go on a quick trip to Vinada," Ki told them when the meal was done. "I need a pair of jeans or two, I think."

"Keep your eyes peeled," Ferguson advised. "The jiggers who tried what they did last night won't stop at anything, that I think."

"I'll be back before dark," Ki promised, and left.

Jessie relaxed with another cup of coffee, then said, "Ian, I'd like to take a little ride over our range. Will you join me?"

Ferguson grinned boyishly and accepted her suggestion with alacrity. "I'll find the time. Wild horses couldn't stop me."

Shortly they went and saddled up, Ferguson leaving High-pocket to finish lining out the crew and getting the work routine back to normal. After leaving the fenced yard, they made good progress across the bench west of where the ranch sat. Soon they were paralleling the depression of the desert, overlooking it from an elevation a half mile or so to the north. About the time they spotted the tall derricks that marked the oil field, they angled right, toward the better graze, which Ferguson said lay just beyond the immediate hills.

These were the hills which Broderick Teague had claimed were oddly stratified, indicating oil below their base in the desert. Now, in the daylight, Jessie studied the sections of broken and chopped highlands they were rising through. Her brow furrowed, and after a while she murmured, "Odd . . . Very odd . . ."

"What is?"

"The division between these slopes and the desert rim, Ian. It's as if it'd been chopped along with an ax, and I can't understand the reason for such an abrupt transition."

Ferguson shrugged. "Nature's unpredictable, is all."

Nevertheless, Jessie continued to ponder the cause, while the slopes became steeper and the canyons narrower. Eventually they topped a high ledge, like a short plateau, where they paused for a break and to let their horses get bottom again. From here, they commanded a view southward of the land they'd crossed, the desert beyond, and Cartinas's range yonder in the distance.

As far and high as they were, they could hear the faint whine of derrick ropes, the chugging of bits churning into the sand, and the vibrating pulse of the pumps. Ferguson gazed at the oil field operation and shook his head. "Sure's different now, isn't it?"

"Well, progress is apt to be noisy and active."

"Less'n a year ago, it was a whole lotta nothin'. Teague once told me of when it was an inland sea with tall reeds and giant vegetables massed 'round it, where huge monsters, scaled and tailed, used to wallow and fight." Ferguson grinned sheepishly. "I dunno, but Teague oughta. He's been to college."

"Oh, he's right enough," Jessie replied, surveying the terrain. Suddenly she snapped her fingers. "Of course! It's different! The surface contour is like a wedge channeling toward the desert. But the hills are different. They're higher here than on the other side."

"Jessie, what'n blazes are you talking about?"

"Cartinas's hills are lower, rounder, from being weathered down longer. They're a lot older than these, which must be a comparatively new formation. There must've been a gigantic upheaval here, and this range was thrust up, creating a high wall of a shoreline and buckling so hard that it caused a great fault, which is now the desert. There would've been the sinking of a wide area to the south, I figure, and those hills would've become tops of islands. And because of this massive shift, this tilting of slope, the sea would've drained southward, where it would've remained in pools and marshy lagoons long after the water in the desert had evaporated."

"So?"

"So, a few hundred million years ago, Cartinas's spread was an inland sea, while the desert had dried to salt. I'm willing to bet a hatful of dollars that despite how the present land surface appears, the general underground stratum still tends toward the south."

"Well, I won't argue, but Teague might. He swears the sea was only where the desert is, and down there is where all the oil is. Calls it scientific analysis or natural conditions, or somesuch."

Jessie turned in her saddle to favor Ferguson with a long stare, eyes thoughtful. "Yes, he should know," she said at last.

They rode on in silence for several miles. They would dip through one scrub-clogged canyon and then up to crown some barren crag, only to encounter another canyon, with yet another crag looming beyond that. Gradually, however, the winding canyons grew shallow and the ridges more rounded, and finally they moved out across a wide, gently rolling pastureland.

At length Ferguson slowed the pace. Jessie glanced ahead expectantly, and as she did, a large brownish bird flew up from some underbrush, flapped heavily over the trees, and vanished. When the riders advanced, Jessie was soon conscious of a horrid odor.

"Something's rotting," she said, wrinkling her nose.

"What, again?" Anxiously, Ferguson spurred forward.

A moment later, Jessie sighted strands of barbed wire barring the way. They pulled up outside the wire, which

82

had been clipped and torn aside, near the edge of a wide and fairly deep bowl-shaped hollow. The sides of the hollow were clotted with bushes and weeds, for at the bottom was a spring of water, fringed with rushes. Crisscrossing the floor of the hollow, this way and that, were ledges of broken and fissured rock. Between them wound a number of animal paths leading to the water.

It was a weird place in itself, but what it contained made it seem nightmarish. Scattered over the floor were the picked and decaying carcasses of numerous cattle. Feasting on the carrion were clouds of vultures.

Jessie gasped, revolted. Ferguson whistled under his breath, his face grim as he gestured at the scene of death and putrefaction.

"Yesterday," he said. "Maybe the rustlers last night."

Jessie nodded. "Not long, anyway. Poisoned?"

"Undoubtedly. You could see the same at the other waterholes, when arsenic was dumped in 'em. Damn! I fenced the holes and try to have 'em patrolled reg'larly, but despite my precautions..." He left the sentence unfinished, his eyes brooding.

They skirted the hollow and kept on across the rolls of land, where sage claimed the thin, rocky soil on the high spots, and grass grew lush in the pockets where winter runoffs deposited richer soil. And over everything was the bright red-gold sheen of the sun, which was already hot and blistering.

Cattle were clustered under shade and by other sources of water, giving Jessie a chance to look over the stock as they rode. For the most part the cows were in good shape, fleshed solid and holding their weight well. But the summer season had been long and hot, and there was the ever-present danger of heel flies. They'd lose what tallow they had gained and the meat would be stringy and the price would drop. It was time for a fall gather, time to get them moving.

When a faint echoing murmur of hoofbeats suddenly reached them, Ferguson reared alertly. "Somebody's following us," he said.

Jessie nodded. "Somebody's about, anyway. Our hands?"

"Shouldn't be, not o'er here at this hour."

The only visible indication of the riders was a wispy smudge of dust rising against the sky. Glancing behind her at it, Jessie said, "I don't know if they're after us, or merely heading in this direction."

"Well, let's see if they dog our steps."

Goading their mounts into a spritely trot, Jessie and Ferguson curved across the open until they intercepted a cattle trail, taking it easterly as it meandered through a succession of interconnecting valleys and canyons. Often they checked their backtrail, but there was no sign of pursuit. Once they stopped and dimly heard the riders.

After three or so miles, they cut away from the trail and reined in by a small rill. Nearby, where cottonwoods stood gnarled and twisted in their patches of velvet shade, hunkered a square cabin built of bricks spaded from the earth rather than molded and dried. It had no windows, but had a veritable portal of a front door, and a stable of sorts attached to one side, and a pitched-roof attic barn and hayloft. Such combinations in single dwellings were odd to see but not uncommon, many landowners lacking the money or need for separate structures. Helluva way to live, though.

They dismounted, stiff and tired. Gratefully their horses sunk muzzles to water and fringing scratch-grass. Jessie and Ferguson joined the horses in drinking the water, though for them there was no food. Afterwards, they tied the horses out of sight in the stable, removed carbines, and went into the house.

Essentially, the interior was a kitchen with a bunk in one corner. Dingy cabinets, chairs and table; cobwebbed walls and ceiling; lots of ratdroppings on the bare floor; and a cannonball stove with a skillet and coffee pot on it. It smelled of rancid cooking grease.

"Let's go up to the hayloft," Ferguson said.

"Think it's safe?" Jessie teased, climbing a slat ladder nailed to the wall and coming up into the loft. It was dark, but she could feel the spongy smattering of leftover hay spread around the floor.

Ferguson, following her up, crossed to open the outer loft door about six inches. They could see partly past the front corner of the cabin, toward the cottonwoods and the creek. On the sill before them, they laid out their carbines and revolvers, and then they stretched flat on the matted hay, their faces together at the door crack.

"I reckon we got a pretty long wait," Ferguson said.

That was fine with Jessie. The day was warm and the air very still, lulling her with an aura of tranquility. She knew they were here as a precaution, to find out if they were being trailed and, if so, by whom—she also doubted they were, and felt here was one of those quiet eddies of relaxation which seldom came into her life.

"Certainly is peaceful, Ian, wherever we are."

"The Garcia homestead, Felix Garcia being the previous owner of your ranch. I was planning to take you here anyway. It's the only shack in this whole section, so we left it up, and all of us use it for shelter and stopovers as the case may be."

Jessie shifted her body and reflexively Ferguson touched her. They lay prone that way for quite a while, aware of each other and stirred by the closeness and the knowing. Jessie could feel his breath against her face and smell the fragrance of his masculine body...and gradually, against her will, she sensed stewing tendrils of pleasure beginning to curl in her belly and loins, and she clenched her buttocks in a futile attempt to quell them.

Ferguson felt her tensing and touched her again as though he thought she were fearful and needed reassuring. She caught his hand in her own, the gentle caress of her fingers like a magnetic contact. It aroused desires long dormant and now her face was close, so that there was a blending of warm eyes and ripe lips and clean-scented hair.

"They're green," he mused, gazing into her eyes. "Imogene's were blue." Then, self-consciously impelled to explain, he added, "Sorry, I'm not over her death. I'll always love my wife."

"We all have loves to remember, Ian."

The thrusting impulse to take Jessie in his arms was elemental, without conscious thought or effort. It was as natural as breathing. He just reached out and drew her to him and kissed her in the deliberate fashion of a man savoring a cherished delicacy. There was a fleeting moment when the sweet flavor of her lips swept him reeling, beyond regard for who and what she was, the boss lady. Then he released her.

His voice was husky, choking. "An accident. Won't happen again. I apologize. No, by God, it was too delicious for me to be sorry."

Expecting indignation, Ferguson saw an obscure amusement soften the contours of her face. Her lips, very red from recent kissing, eased into a slow smile and she purred, "Then I'm not sorry for it, either." Impishly, she kissed him back on the mouth. "Or for that, Ian."

Provoked by her taunting intimacies, Ferguson pushed her down on the hay in a strong embrace, feeling her breasts pulsing against him through her blouse. He moved his hands over the silken fabric, sensing the warmth of her skin and wishing he could run his fingers across her naked flesh, yet fearing to ask and offend her. They continued kissing with increased fervor, his passion mounting until—

"Naked," he gasped, "I want you naked..."

Jessie murmured assent. "You, too."

Ferguson fumbled hurriedly to strip off his clothes. Jessie gazed at him, her lips glistening, a smoky glow in her eyes as she shucked bare and stretched out on the straw, swollen breasts throbbing, curvaceous hips slackly apart, her tender self exposed invitingly.

Now also nude, Ferguson eased alongside her and hovered with both hands prowling over her breasts and nipples. Jessie squirmed, sighing, his touches igniting her... and then she shuddered as he dipped his head down to her trembling belly and tongued her navel. She whimpered, tangling her fingers in his hair while his tongue moved farther down and thrust deep, teasing her delicate flesh and tasting her loins. Her thighs clenched spasmodically around his laving tongue and nibbling lips, excitement spiraling up inside her.

Ferguson eased his tongue along her cleft, swirling back and forth across her most sensitive area. Jessie sucked in her breath, exhaling sharply in response to his suckling mouth, spearing tongue, and nipping teeth. A minute...two minutes...her belly rippled. She began to pant explosively, her hips curving up, her pelvis grinding against his face with pulsating tension...

And Jessie climaxed, wailing, twisting in the clutch of her sweet agony. She shivered and relaxed...or *tried* to relax, as Ferguson continued his darting like summer lightning against her moist pink flesh, and she felt herself building to another crest.

"That—that's enough . . . I'm ready . . . Now, now . . ."

Ferguson rose and knelt over her. She lay silent with anticipation, her legs spread on either side of him, her exposed center moist and throbbing. He levered downward, and she groaned with the rock-hard feel of him as he began his penetrating entry. She pushed upward, her thighs clasping him, swallowing his full thick length inside her eager belly, her muscles squeezing around him so tightly that he nearly cried out.

He thrust, then, and she automatically responded in rhythm, mewing deep in her throat, her splayed thighs arching spasmodically against his pumping hips. He licked her cheek and laved her ear. Then their mouths touched, pressing together with lips apart and tongues intertwining. Their tempo increased and increased again to a greedy pace, their naked flesh frantic in their pummeling madness. Ferguson's breath rasped in his throat; Jessie's legs cramped where they gripped his middle. There was nothing but exquisite sensation, no existence beyond the boundaries of their bodies.

Then Jessie felt him grow even larger in his pre-orgasmic surge, saw his eyes sparkle with lust, and felt his tension and quickening motions. Ferguson's final, bruising thrusts triggered her release again. She moaned, sobbing, as her second climax overwhelmed her, nails raking, her limbs jerking violently.

"Ahhhh . . . !"

She felt Ferguson's release, felt his juices spewing hot within. She absorbed all of his flowing passion, until, with a final convulsion, she lay still, satiated. She sighed, thinking about asking him to stop . . . but then she felt his shaft regaining hardness and girth, felt him reviving his gentle drumming of her loins.

"Lord, don't you ever get enough?"

He chuckled lewdly. "Practice makes perfect."

Despite being drained and lethargic, Jessie found herself beginning to respond, gliding along the length of his resurgent shaft, her inner self tingling with each pushing impact against his pelvic bone. She closed her eyes, feeling herself rekindle inside—

Then raucous voices and galloping hooves sounded outside the hayloft door. The sensual spell shattered, Ferguson jackknifed off Jessie's loins. Equally startled, Jessie twisted, pivoting in a crouch, hearing the approaching shouts and horses and, above those now, the sharp bursts of gunfire. They peered outside.

"Migawd!" Ferguson blurted. "It's Alice, bein' chased!" He scooped up a carbine, hopped on one leg. "You're steppin' on my pants!"

"You got my gun!" Jessie retorted, frenziedly scurrying.

Eight riders were plunging toward the cabin, breaking from the cattle trail beyond the rill and cottonwood grove. Ahead by mere heartbeats, Alice was twisted in her saddle and firing a lady's-weight .31 Colt at her pursuers, but with no success, the rough gallop and awkward position making effective aim impossible. Then, her pistol snapping empty, she shifted forward, hugging her horse, and headed for the cabin—the only place for miles, she knew, to find shelter and stand off a seige.

Sunrays flashed off gunmetal as the seven horsemen shot while they chased her. Swaying and jouncing in their saddles, they were no more accurate than she'd been, their bullets flying high and wide. But up in the hayloft, Jessie and Ferguson were able to draw swift yet steady beads. Blasts snarled back through the narrow room as they each triggered once. Outside, one man either fell or dived off his horse.

"You got him," Ferguson said. "A real meat-in-the-pot shot."

"Not me. You did," Jessie countered, relevering. "It doesn't matter who did. Cover your girl; she's coming in fast!"

Bracketed by their whining slugs, Alice neared and dismounted at a run. Behind her, the charging men were scattered by raking bullets from the loft, only to wheel circling and attack at wide angles, revolvers bucking, lead searching for the two above.

The flimsy front stoop trembled under the pound of the gunmen's boots. The leading man, armed, opened the door and, crouched, scanned the room. "Near the ladder! There's the bitch; get her!" he yelled. "And get them bastards holed upstairs, too!"

He sprang for Alice, tripping, and skidded flat when she sledged him alongside his jaw with a skillet. A renegade flung past him and leaped to grab the skillet as well as the girl. The next instant he stopped as if he had slammed into an invisible wall.

From near the top of the ladder, muzzle flame had stabbed at him. And Jessie's trim figure hurtled down the steps to get in another shot with her pistol, just in time to see Alice elude the grasping clutch of a third brute. The girl had snatched out a small but keen-edged knife from her boot and was warily maneuvering along her side of the heavy kitchen table, across which she was fending off the brutal hands of her assailant. Jessie ducked to one side, pivoting to fire—then ducked aside again, evading gunfire from the other men, who were piling in, swarming around their falling, dying comrades.

Ian Ferguson's raging shout came from above—and so did he, launching from the loft and dropping to roll over and over, while slugs dug viciously in the floor. He fired as he rolled, and one of the charging gunmen stumbled and grabbed at a wounded side as he crumpled.

The burly man after Alice lunged headlong across the top of the table toward her, disdainful of a female's ability to wield a knife. And for his trouble, Alice laid the flesh of one cheek and the muscle of one arm open to the bone with two quick and skillful strokes. A roar of pain and rage crossed the man's lips as he hit the floor on the far side of the table. He reared upright, his face gory with his own blood and one arm hanging uselessly, yet his other hand managed to grab Alice as she dodged, and to rip the knife from her fist.

Alice screamed. Two other gunmen swiveled her way. Their fire and that from Jessie's custom .38 seemed to intermesh. One of the men buckled in the middle and collapsed on his nose. The other reeled doorward, blood fountaining from his severed aorta. Another scream from Alice, this one drowned by Jessie's third shot, which was fired a hairsbreadth past the girl, Jessie knowing she must cut the burly man down before he could strike.

The gleaming boot knife whipped back and then forward toward its mark before Jessie's bullet even hit him. The man stumbled sideways under its impact, blood spurting from his neck and abruptly dying the shoulder of his shirt a deep red blue. His hand began to wobble slowly, half shaking as if it were trying to deny the fatal wound. Then he crumpled. It was all in half a second.

The two gunmen, still alive, lunged for the door, one clasping his smashed arm, the other cupping his shattered jaw. They barged outside and went speedily dashing for their horses, firing a few haphazard shots to cover their flight.

Jessie and Ferguson would have gone after them, but Alice needed attention. Her slim-bladed knife had missed her heart, for which the dead killer had plainly intended it, but it had sliced through the flesh of Alice's shoulder, below the collarbone, and pinned her to the cabinets behind. Her face had paled, and her eyes were tensely squeezed, glassy with pain.

While Ferguson held his daughter steady, Jessie removed the knife. Alice clenched her teeth as she fought off a faint, but the pain and shock were too much for her. Gently her father gathered the unconscious girl in his arms and crossed the few steps to the table. At the moment it seemed the handiest place to dress her wound.

As he freed his arms of her weight, they heard the wild, rapid drumming of horses fading away in the distance. "They're gone," Jessie said, picking up the fallen coffee pot. "I'll fetch some water and try to get the old stove going to boil it. In any case, she's going to need more than we can do here, Ian. She's going to need doctor's tending, soon as possible."

"Then we'll take her straight to Doc Egger," Ferguson replied distraughtly. "The ride from here is a tad longer to town than back to the ranch, but it'll save time rather than gettin' and bringin' him."

There was no further discussion.

Chapter 7

Earlier that same day, Ki reached Vinada without incident and hitched his horse at a convenient rack. He went across to the general store and bought a couple of pairs of jeans, but his purchase was as much an excuse to talk as it was for need of new pants. In fact, the main reason he'd come to town was to gain information.

On the surface, it appeared as though the Cartinases had cause to label the oil workers as troublemakers. The rainshed around the desert field was dying fast and was soaked with oil, no mistake about that. Yet those rustlers last night had worked as cowhands at sometime or other, Ki felt sure, even if that greasy pocket tied one rider to the wells now. Moreover, Jessie's water supplies were being deliberately poisoned by someone who knew how to use arsenic—enough to kill, but not too much to scare off the cattle—and that implied someone with rangeland experience. The arsenic had to've been bought someplace. If Ki could get a line on a gent who'd made a considerable purchase of late, he'd have, he hoped, something to go on.

Having no luck at the general store, Ki continued his inquiries around the plaza, buying when necessary some cheap item in order to strike up a conversation. By the time he'd returned to his horse, however, he'd discovered nothing, absolutely nothing new. So his next step, he figured, was to see what might be seen in the saloons.

And of the saloons, the foremost was the Oasis.

He entered the establishment and found it to be a scene of contrasts. The woodwork was raw and unpainted, the long bar of roughly planed planks, yet the tables and chairs were polished smooth with age and use, and the back bar mirror was genuine French plate. Bottles of every shape and color pyramided the back bar, and the lunch counter over to one side gleamed with copper and glass.

Ki pushed his way to the bar and then waited, the bartenders busy serving customers before him. Most of this early crowd were oil workers, he noted, but there was a sprinkling of cowhands and several who looked like cowhands but weren't. Ki studied the hard-faced lookalikes, trying to recall any from last night's rustling crew. When his beer had been served and he was lifting it, he chanced to spot a couple of men among those playing stud poker at a rear table, and an intuitive sense of recognition sparked through him, even though consciously he couldn't identify them for sure.

Intrigued, Ki observed them gambling. He always watched in the mirror, so he did not have to turn around. They were bleach-eyed jiggers, tight of mouth and long on twist, who sipped their whiskeys, played lackadaisically, and generally acted as men might when bored.

They stayed at it, though, glancing frequently at the patrons coming and going, and at the wall clock mounted beside the fancy back bar.

It was a lengthy wait. Ki nursed another beer, and the clock chimed two o'clock before two men cashed in and left the table. They glided past Ki, who carefully kept his back to them, went outside with nary a backward glance, and then turned left up the boardwalk.

Moving quickly, but in a way that would attract no special attention, Ki followed them. He felt they were familiar, but he still couldn't tell precisely why—yet instinct was sufficient; Ki was puzzled and meant to discover the answer. Walking swiftly, the pair went along the plaza to the Poinsettia Hotel, which was a fairly compact two-story home that had been converted into a boarding house type of arrangement. Ki, tracking like a shadow, saw them go in the Poinsettia's front door, then glimpsed them through the lobby windows as they nodded to someone—a desk clerk?—and climbed a flight of stairs to the second floor.

Ki took a chance and hurried along the side of the hotel, encountering no one. He reached a rear door, found it unlocked, and located a set of back steps at the end of a short hallway. Quickly, quietly he went up, aware he was taking precious time and probably some risk, but knowing his hunch was too strong to ignore.

The second floor corridor was empty at the moment. He padded along the hall, trying to avoid loose, creaky boards while keeping alert for sounds from any of the rooms. Abruptly he paused, hearing voices through the thin panels of the door just ahead. The front stairs were only a few steps away, and Ki had to keep an eye on them and listen in case somebody opened a door to emerge from another room. He strained to make sense of the muffled talk—curious talk, which told Ki enough to bring a faster flow of blood through his veins, but not enough to give him any real knowledge of the phantom of violence plaguing the region.

"Glad Latham's over there now," he heard a man's voice say. "We lost our shirts in that stud game, and for what? Nothin'."

"Still cheaper paying your losses this way, than for you to be boozing it up while you wait around," another man growled, his voice more authoritarian and with a slight gutteral inflection. Ki tried to identify it, but the voice was too low and filtered for him to discern whether the accent was foreign, regional, or from some speech defect. "Here, this should cover them. And maybe it was for nothing this time. He's bound to hit town very soon; he's got no alternative, and we've got to be ready—and sober—when he shows up."

Now he heard the sound of coins and a third voice chuckling. "Yeah, that fool'll run 'round like a blind dog in a butcher shop. Keep the pennies. We're fair enough long's you play fair with us."

"Fair! Why, I ought to dock you scarecrows for having bungled your job last night," the second man retorted. "What a hellish mess!"

"We done the best we could. The bunch of us tangled our loop a little, I guess, but it was the boss who told us where to drive and leave that herd. We gotta have more men," the first man argued nervously. "We gotta have enough to win any fight that comes at us."

"It's like I've been tellin' you all along," the third man insisted, as if agreeing with the first man's demand, "there's too much at stake to keep on pussy-footin' around. Only the boss is so anxious that nobody find out about us, about the plans, for fear some o' the crowd he hob-

96

nobs with would think he weren't respectable—"

"Dry it!" the surly-voiced man snarled. "None of that concerns none of you. Just keep your mind on your own job and get it done right or I'll kill you so damned quick it'll be like blowing out a light."

"You can, I know. You've killed good men in the past, but it don't pay to wipe out your own gunbuzzards— 'specially right when you're apt to be needin' 'em the most. We don't cotton to threats."

"Oh, damn that! Sit down, have a drink, boys. I'm just keyed up because I'm not finished with them—nor with her either, yet."

Suddenly Ki glimpsed the top of a Stetson between the banisters of the front stairs. Hastily he retreated along the corridor to the rear steps, going down a few and then flattening to the stairwell wall, holding his breath. Hollow bootfalls sounded as the hat's owner reached the second floor landing and crossed the hall. He knocked on a door; there was a buzzing of voices and the closing of a door. Now, obviously, a fourth man had joined the other three.

Ki continued on down the steps and out the rear door of the hotel. Snooping around that room had become too risky, and besides, he was more interested now in seeing who was talking, not merely hearing them. So he made his way back to the plaza, sauntered diagonally across to where he had a good view of the front of the hotel, and waited for any or all of the men to leave.

Less than ten minutes passed when three different men came out of a small house two doors up from the hotel. Among them Ki recognized Ev Moran, his nose heavily taped with fresh bandages. The stony trio eyed him speculatively as they headed toward the Oasis.

Another five minutes passed. An untidy, corpulent

woman hurried up to that same house, pounded excitedly on the door, and waddled inside. A moment later she reappeared, followed by a rather tall, frockcoated man with a cadaverous face and the kind of black cabinet bag carried by doctors. Ki barely escaped a collision with the woman as she trundled by, the doctor in tow. "He's sayin' she's his wife, but I ne'er saw them afore and she's beaten him with a bedpan," the woman was sputtering, her multiple chins quivering with outrage.

Her snippet of juicy gossip almost piqued Ki's curiosity enough to tag behind, but he didn't. He stayed put and was still watching the hotel a good twenty minutes later when Jessie and Ferguson rode into town. Ferguson was supporting Alice, who was carrying herself sidewise against him, her left shoulder and upper arm bandaged in knotted strips of his shirt, then cloaked by his jacket.

As they reined in by the doctor's house, Ki began running. So did a man wearing a badge on his vest— Sheriff Wexler, Ki assumed, the lawman appearing to be in his fifties, but still hardy and sharp, with iron-gray whiskers bracketing his florid face. The sheriff came from across the plaza, where he'd just turned from a side street in the company of Broderick Teague. Teague also broke into a nimble sprint, catching up and helping the sheriff elbow through the gathering crowd of gawpers.

"My child's been knifed," Ferguson replied to the volley of questions and explained in terse sentences how it had come about.

"The ornery polecats!" Sheriff Wexler stormed. "Happen on a purty gal and figure to kill her if'n they can't foul her, eh?"

Weakly Alice agreed, wincing as she slipped from the saddle with her father. "I . . . guess that's it. I was just trying to find Papa and Jessie . . . to join them, and crossed paths with those awful men. Couldn't outrun them, knew only one place to hide . . . Was lucky . . ."

Teague nodded soulfully. "Now, to Dr. Egger with you."

"He's out," Ki said. "I saw him leave on foot awhile ago."

"Means he's probably somewhere here in town. I'll find him," Wexler stated, "but meantime, Alice needs a place to rest and wait."

"My home. Plenty of room. Why, she'll have more comfort and attention than she'll know what to do with," Teague boasted.

His offer was the best choice and was gratefully accepted. A blanket litter was rigged so that Alice could be transported with minimal pain, and a small crowd trailed at a discreet distance as the grim cavalcade left the plaza and marched to Teague's big house.

Once inside, Alice was carried up to a spare bedroom and delivered into the sympathetically clucking custody of Teague's two housemaids. They were plain, good-hearted women of middle age who had Alice under the covers and sipping beef and herb broth before the poor girl could properly thank them.

Soon the cadaverous-faced doctor hurried in. He nodded to Ferguson and the others and instantly went to Alice, whose face was drawn, her eyes still brassy with that look of hurting distress.

"All right, it's my turn to play sawbones," Doc Egger said, as he opened his bag and began rummaging about. "Outside, everybody."

They all left the room, closing the door and trooping downstairs. Doc Egger worked on Alice for some time. Finally he appeared, descending with a sigh, daubing his forehead with a kerchief.

"Well, I cleansed the wound and sewed it up some," he told the others, "and she's drifted into a natural sleep. I'm satisfied with her appearance and don't believe any infection has set in."

"Thanks, Doc. Soon's she awakens, I'll take her—"

"Wouldn't advise taking her anywhere, Ian, not quite yet. Apt to pull her stitches like the tophem of a feed sack, if she moves much."

"Then I insist she makes my home her hospice," Teague declared quickly, going on though Ferguson began to shake his head no. "My servants complain endlessly because they've nothing to occupy their time except looking after me. It'll be like a gift to them—having Alice to fuss over while she recuperates."

"P'raps so, Broderick, but you know how folks are about, er, convention, that sort of thing." Ferguson frowned, shaking his head. "It's foolish, but some of 'em would be sure to rumor-monger, and I can't stick around here, not with a ranch I gotta keep runnin'."

"I could stay for a while," Jessie suggested.

"Do, please," Teague urged, not quite as enthusiastically.

"In a day or so Alice should be strong enough to travel," Doc Egger said. "Just keep her quiet. I'll drop by tomorrow."

While Teague escorted the doctor to the door, Ki remarked quietly, "Friend Broderick didn't sound thrilled about your chaperoning, Jessie."

She regarded Ki quizzically. "Does he worry you somehow?"

Ki was about to respond, when Ferguson muttered, "He worried you earlier, him claiming only the desert had been under water."

"Not worried, Ian; he merely caused one to wonder.

100

Stop acting like a fretful parent," Jessie scolded, folding her arms. "Oil exploration is Broderick's specialty, not mine. Father never found him wrong in that or in any other way, and I'm sure I won't either."

Ki shrugged. "Things change. People change. For all the bond that was between the two of them, your father and Teague, it might be a bond that doesn't extend beyond that. Not even to you, Jessie."

"Might be," she allowed without conviction, and then Teague returned, and the conversation switched. Soon Ki and Ferguson bade their good-byes, leaving Teague and Jessie at the house.

"She's right, y'know," Ferguson said, as they walked back to the plaza. "Teague is okay. I'm just upset and bein' too protective. Hard not to be, Alice bein' motherless and so innocent and all."

Ki nodded noncommittally. "You ready to ride on home now?"

"Well, there're some errands I should do first. Can't say I'm in much mood for them. A coupla stiff snorts would be more like it."

"I'll buy you one at the Oasis when you're done."

"You got a deal, Ki. I'll meet you there in short order."

They parted, and Ki went to the popular saloon again. If he'd had his druthers, he'd have scouted around the Poinsettia Hotel some more, but the situation there was anybody's guess now. Also, he didn't have much time, and he didn't want Ferguson accidentally interfering. Ferguson was wound up too tight for Ki to trust his judgment.

The Oasis, though, was the next best choice to visit. From the conversation he'd overheard, Ki gathered the two men he'd trailed to the hotel had been staked out in the saloon for some crooked purpose, and that another man named Latham had remained after they'd left. It wasn't much, but worth checking out. Besides, Ki was hungry.

He bought another beer, took a boiled egg and a sandwich from the free lunch counter, then sought out a chair near the gambling tables. He found one toward the back, next to the side wall. Up along the wall was a row of antlers from deer and other game animals, the horns being used as hooks for numerous coats and jackets. Ki shifted his chair away from the hanging garments so he could get a better view of the players at the card tables, studying them without appearing to, while drinking his beer and eating his food.

The pair he'd followed were nowhere around, nor was anybody wearing the Stetson he'd seen bobbing on the hotel stairs. And if Latham or others of his ilk were there, they weren't broadcasting their presence. But Ki did spot Ev Moran and his two sidekicks, playing draw poker with four other guys. Watching, Ki got the impression that Moran was simply taking a break before returning to work, more interested in relaxing than in concentrating on the game.

Ki was just finishing his sandwich when Moran and his pals left the table, having more or less broken even. They headed toward Ki, moving to take their coats from the racks almost behind him, not speaking to him but raking him with intolerant eyes. Ki peeled his egg, ignoring them. They shrugged on their coats, then Moran hesitated, scowling, and focused acutely on Ki for an instant.

"Sonuvabitch," Moran growled. With him leading, they clumped across to where a black-coated bouncer stood by the bar and engaged him in hushed conversation. Occasionally they shot glances in Ki's direction. Ki tapped salt on his egg and ate it in three bites.

Finally Moran turned and strode back, his followers fanning out on either side of him. The bouncer remained at the bar, very alert. A few feet from Ki's table the group paused, Moran staring truculently.

"Some bastard stole my wallet, you."

Ki smiled. "Are you talking to me?"

"My good leather wallet, right outta my jacket."

"Sorry to hear that." Ki licked his fingers and smiled again. A hush had abruptly developed, broken here and there by the scrape of a booted heel as the patrons kept easing aside to make room. Some of the women who'd been dancing or lining the long bar to wheedle drinks were already turning and scooting to safer spots. They knew, as did the men, that trouble would not be long coming.

Ev Moran's face darkened. "I've had all the truck I'm taking from you. You got two seconds to cough up my wallet, y'hear that?"

Ki lost his smile. "I didn't take your wallet."

From the sidelines, a customer who'd been sitting at Ki's table called out, "The feller didn't even touch your coat, Moran. He—" But he was cut off by Moran, who snarled, "You used some kind of jiggery-pokery, but your sly tricks don't fool me. One second left."

The two ranch hands hunched in alongside Moran, the same hard, suspicious antagonism on their faces. Ki leaned back in his chair, outwardly calm as he eyed them and measured Moran's ultimatum, but feeling his anger welling up inside. The smart move would be to crawfish, even if it meant stripping down to prove he wasn't hiding Moran's wallet. It'd be crazy to antagonize Moran further, to invite a barroom brawl and possible injury, and to worsen relations between the two ranches. On the other hand, Moran was asking for it.

"Ev," Ki said amiably, "go stuff your wallet."

Bellowing, Moran lunged over the table for Ki. Ki sprang backward out of his chair, and the table collapsed under Moran's wild dive. Instead of reaching for a weapon, Ki swivelled and, as Moran stumbled off balance, he planted a foot where the wallet should have been and shoved. Moran lurched head-on into the next table, snapping it like kindling.

"I'll rip you apart for this!" Moran yelled, getting to his feet. Ki only grinned coldly, picking up a broken table leg and swinging it about, keeping the ranch hands at bay as they tried to close in and trip him or hit him when his back was turned. Moran came at him like a buffalo, and stepping aside at the last moment, Ki bopped Moran on the head with the leg, shattering the leg useless and sending Moran stumbling across and into the massive plank bar.

The entire length of the bar shuddered and almost toppled over. Moran bounded back as if nothing had collided, the white nose plaster contrasting brightly with his scarlet face. He barked an oath. His right hand thrust for his holster. Then he froze, gripping the butt of his Smith & Wesson. His two crewmen also stood rigid, hands close to their belts, but making no move to draw. They were all staring at the curve-bladed knife and the throwing dagger that just seemed to happen into Ki's hands, ready to be flung.

Both a gun and a knife could draw blood and create fear. But however brave with a gun, cowpokes generally regarded a naked blade in close conflict with the same fear and loathing felt toward a venomous snake—both were so silent, swift, and lethal that they could spark primitive terror and inspire one hell of a lot of cooperation. Yet not everyone there was fully intimidated.

Ki's left arm snapped in a blur; a sliver of metal winked in the lamplight. A pistol blazed fire across the room, drowning out a howl of pain as the bouncer reeled against the bar, pawing at his bloodied hand. The stubby-barreled hideout gun he'd stealthily drawn clattered to the floor from nerveless fingers, the web of his thumb and much of his palm skewered by an unerringly tossed dagger.

Another dagger was already balanced in Ki's left hand. His eyes and that dagger seemed to cover the whole room and single out each man there for special and individual attention. The longer blade of his delicately curved *tanto* still poised unwaveringly at Ev Moran and his ranch hands.

"You can't get away with it," Moran said thickly.

"I'm not trying to get away with anything," Ki replied pointedly. "It was you boys who tried to get away with something. What authority have you got to accuse me of theft and threaten me when I deny it?"

Moran swallowed, rage almost choking him. He was about to respond when a harsh voice rang from the saloon's entry.

"What gives in here?"

Sheriff Wexler strode inside, his star of office gleaming on his sagging vest, a cocked shotgun nestled in the crook of his arm. "Well? Speak up, who started this ruckus? You," he snapped at Ki, "pen them stickers. If there's any slingin' to be done hereabouts, I'll do it with my double-ought."

Ki obediently sheathed his *tanto* and dagger, righted his chair, and resumed his seat as if nothing had occurred. The sheriff stared at him, his whiskers twitching slightly. Moran found his voice.

"He swiped my wallet," he charged, pointing at Ki.

"How's that? Where?"

"Here!" Moran flapped open his jacket, showing his empty inside pockets. "It was hot in here, so I took off my coat and hung it on that horn there. Well, after we finished playin' cards I put it back on and discovered my wallet was missing. And him—Ki—he was sitting almost underneath where my coat was hung."

Wexler showed concern. "Lose much money?"

"Nope, didn't lose any money. Never pack money in that wallet, just some papers. But it was a big wallet and looked fat, and I betcha this sonuvabitch must've figured I carried lots of *dinero* in it."

"Uh-huh. Important papers?"

"Oh, important enough, authorizings and delivery bonuses and stuff like that. But they can be replaced or managed without."

Wexler turned to Ki. "Whatcha got to say for yourself?"

"I'm not hiding a big, fat wallet." Rising, Ki opened his vest and slowly pivoted, then indicated his witness. "Ask him about it."

Again the customer defended Ki. "Didn't see nobody else lift nothing, neither. Course, I sat down only a few minutes before him."

Sheriff Wexler called out for anyone who knew anything, but nobody owned up. He gave a snort and eyed Moran disparagingly. "The thief's skedaddled, Ev, and chances are he's dumped your wallet somewhere. In any case, you ain't got no call to've accused this man."

"You ain't got no call to side with him!" Moran retorted.

"I'm sidin' with nobody! I'm sworn to uphold the law without fear or favor, and that's what I aim to do." The sheriff turned then to the bouncer. "Horned in, did you, Moody," he stated firmly.

"I just wanted to get the drop," Moody grumbled. He'd removed Ki's dagger and was winding a handkerchief around his hand. "My mistake. I should've stepped in earlier and came a-shootin'."

"And gone out on a shutter," Wexler countered dryly. "Okay, we've had enough of this. Moran, you and your hands were preparin' to leave, so hie on out of here. And Moody, you tend to keepin' the order and not to stirrin' up more disorder." He bent his cold gaze on Ki. "As for you, mister, you keep your nose clean. I won't stand for no promiscuous whittlin' hereabouts. You're salty, all right, but you're not big enough to buck the law any more than anybody else is."

Ki leveled his gaze to meet that of the gruff lawman. "I've no intention of trying," he said quietly, and then, over Wexler's shoulder, he glimpsed Ferguson entering. He waved him to come over.

Instead, Ferguson halted by the door. He gaped at the smashed furniture, the encircling crowd, the shotgun-toting sheriff, and the savagely glowering Moran and his men. "It must've been a devil of a powwow," he murmured. He stood rooted, shaking his head. "If it's all the same to you, Ki," he said in a louder voice, "I think I've just lost my thirst."

Chapter 8

Leaving Vinada, they headed ranchward.

It was a monotonous ride over familiar terrain with the sun burning their backs as it dipped toward evening. Ferguson got a laugh out of Ki's story of the saloon altercation, and later he tried to explain Jessie's theory about the prehistoric lay of the land, only to grow confused and lamely give up. After that, conversation was sporadic and desultory, Ferguson keeping mainly to his thoughts.

Ki honored Ferguson's silence and refrained from intruding, even though for some time he had been eyeing with interest a dark cloud boiling up steadily from the direction of the desert. Then, struck by realization, he said, "Of course! It's a well fire!"

"What? Where?" Ferguson blurted, as though awakening. He stared, giving a low whistle. "You're right. Can't be much else."

"Can't be much worse. A fire in an oil field's a real disaster." Ki lapsed quiet, and for a while they rode gazing at the black plumes roiling up the long slant of sky ahead and at the crimson flare pulsing within the heart of the smoky pall. Finally Ki, rubbing an earlobe, added thoughtfully, "I wonder how it could've started."

"Dang carelessness," Ferguson declared. "But they'll say some cowman or another set it. You just watch if they don't."

"Well, that oil crew didn't strike me as the sort who'd be careless," Ki replied, allowing cryptically. "though I grant it's a great way to stir up trouble, no matter if it happened by accident or was set deliberately. And if it was set, it was a hard chore. You can't fire a well by simply holding a match to it."

Suddenly a heavy eruption quivered the air.

"Now what in tunket!" Ferguson barked.

"Explosives. I'd guess they're trying to blow that burning well and snuff out the fire," Ki said. He stared at the ominous blaze, which billowed higher and thicker than ever. "Doesn't look like they're having much luck with it so far. Probably can't get close enough to place the powder right."

Soon another detonation burst from the desert.

"Still at it," Ferguson commented. "Say, I wouldn't mind amblin' down that way and taking a gander. What about you?"

Ki nodded, grinning.

They spurred southeasterly toward the smoke and fire which marked the scene. More explosives were set off before they arrived, but the blaze continued unabated, consuming the well which had come in and been capped three days before. The platform and partially dismantled derrick were enveloped by a roaring conflagration, the tongues of flame starting a few feet above the mouth of the well and licking high into a gargantuan black cloud, which in turn was glowing darkly as myriad drops of spouting oil were ignited by burning gas.

Some of the workers were engaged in efforts to extinguish the fire, but most were gathered in a turbulent group, pulled far enough back to escape the heat and noxious fumes. Ki and Ferguson reined in near the group—but not so near that it seemed they were interfering—and surveyed the monstrous and baleful red inferno.

Soon the foreman, Vince Handstad, disengaged himself from the group and walked over, tugging the singed ends of his big beard. "Howdy, Ian, Ki," he greeted, his tone as worried as his features. "I was kinda hoping Mr. Teague was with you. Have you seen him?"

"In town," Ferguson said. "He'd be useful 'bout now, eh?"

"Well, he might have some new ideas. None of ours is doing any good. The pressure is mighty low, y'see, allowing the fire and smoke to spread out and preventing us from getting in where we can chuck our blasting sticks into the bore. But we gotta stop it fast."

"Yeah, there's plenty of profits burnin' up there."

Handstad gave Ferguson a scathing look. "Money be damned! Already the well's sump has caught fire, and the way the derrick is sending embers and burning wood all 'round, the other wells and sumps could catch, too. Then there'd be a curtain of fire that'd eat up the entire field." He turned his gaze to the blazing well. "Of all the evenings for the chief not to take his tour," he groaned.

Ki said, "I've got a notion how to put out your fire."

"How's that?" Handstad exclaimed, startled.

"It's a little trick I once saw that worked," Ki elaborated. "I believe I can work it here, but I'll need a few things to do it."

Handstad hesitated, pawing his beard, clearly dubious.

"Better let him have a try," Ferguson prompted. "What've you got to lose, 'cept some more holes blowed in the ground?"

Handstad shrugged. "I dunno . . . but you can't make things any worse, that's for certain. Okay, what kind of stuff do you want?"

"First off, a fairly flexible steel rod about a half inch or three-quarters in diameter and maybe six feet long. Then a file and a coil of fine, strong wire. And I mean *strong*. Oh yes, and several cartridges of blasting powder with some caps and fuse."

"I can get all that, Ki. What else?"

"Some wood saplings or limbs as slender and supple and straight as possible—if they can be found at all in the desert."

"Bit o' luck, there. We've been hauling in trees to saw into logs for our steam engines, and we can forage branches off of them." Handstad hastened back to the group and sent his crew scattering in quest of the needed material. Soon he and the others were returning with all Ki had requested, and they huddled, watching with great interest.

Ki took the file and notched the rod at both ends. He fastened the wire at one end, bent the springy rod into an arc, and secured the other end of the wire. Then he selected the four best branches, cut them into four-foot lengths, scaled off any twigs and excess growth, and carefully notched the smaller end of each slim shaft.

"A bow and arrows," Ferguson said, chuckling. "What're you figuring on doing, Ki, shooting holes in the fire?"

"Something like that," Ki replied with a smile. He chose one of the cartridges and used a length of wire to bind it firmly to the unnotched end of the arrow. "Take the rest of these sticks back a ways. Don't want them lying here if something should go wrong."

"Go wrong!" Handstad erupted. "If the wire breaks or the arrow slips, there won't be enough of you to grease a gunbarrel with!"

"Everything will work out fine," Ki said cheerfully, as he capped the cartridge and secured a very short length of fuse to the cap. He drew his waterproof container of matches from his pocket.

Ferguson paled. "Good God, why not just shoot the damn thing and let the fire light the fuse? It'd be a damn sight safer!"

"Yes, but chances are it'd fail. There's pressure coming out of the well, and the fire is actually several feet above the wellhead. The fuse would hardly light as it whizzed through the flames. The best we could hope for would be to drop it right into the bore, which isn't likely, and at that, the rising gas and oil would toss it out before it could explode." Ki shook his head. "No, the only way is to shoot it in lighted. Now, stand clear, everyone, just in case."

The crewmen retreated hastily. Ferguson paused, then also hurried back, taking their horses with him. Vince Handstad stayed right where he was. Ki glanced at him questioningly.

"You think I'll perch safe while a man risks his life to save my well?" the foreman growled defiantly. "Gimme those matches and I'll light the fuse after you snag the

112

arrow on the string. That'll make it easier and less liable for things to, er, go wrong."

Ki smiled and did not protest. He lifted the notched end of the arrow to the wire and raised the bow. "Powder!" he said.

Handstad struck a match and applied it to the dangling end of the fuse. There was a hiss, a rain of sparks. Ki drew the arrow back its full length, the muscles of his arm and shoulder swelling, for the bow was a stiff one and difficult to bend. The bowstring twanged with a rich, deep hum. The arrow, trailing a spurtle of sparks, soared through the air and vanished into the fiery cloud.

Almost instantly there was an earth-shivering explosion. Smoke and flame flew in every direction with chunks of platform and derrick cascading through the resultant fog.

"You're doin' it!" Handstad whooped. "Look there! The fire is just about half as big as it was! You've nearly got it plugged."

"Another cartridge, somebody!" Ki called out.

Swiftly he readied a second charge. Handstad torched the fuse and Ki strained to draw back on the arrow. With a dull click the wire slipped from the notch and slid down the rod. Handstad gave a yell as the arrow twitched from Ki's fingers and the blasting powder with its sputtering fuse dropped nearby to the ground.

Ki dived for the hissing death, seized the cartridge, and hurtled it toward the well with all his strength. The charge detonated in midair, tumbling Ki and Handstad backward off their feet.

"I must've been loco, agreein' to a fool stunt like this," Handstad gasped as he picked himself up. "Stop it. No more."

"Get me another stick," Ki said adamantly.

113

Handstad wiped sweat from his brow with his sleeve and called for more powder. The watchful group stood silent and rigid as Ki repaired his improvised bow and rigged his third charge.

The fuse was lit and Handstad stood aside, holding his breath while Ki slowly and carefully drew the arrow to a head. The bow twanged, the sputtering cartridge slicing through the air and plunging into the smoke cloud above the well. Straight and true it sped, curving downward at precisely the right instant.

"Got the range now," Ki observed.

The explosion followed his words. And the vacuum created by that ear-ringing explosion cut off the flow of gas for a split second—and as though some massive candle had been snuffed, the fire glowing through the mushroom of black smoke disappeared. The smoke swirled and eddied, then drifted away, revealing a rubbled mass of earth and debris where the wellhead had been, its upper bore caved in and effectively clogged against further leakage.

Cheering, the watchers rushed to congratulate Ki. "Where'd you learn a trick like that?" Ferguson asked, shaking Ki's hand.

"You know, the Indians used to fire buildings with arrows in a similar way."

Ferguson nodded. "Smart thinkin', Ki. Me, I never seen anything even close to such before, have you, Vincent?"

"No," Handstad responded, "and I never want to see it again."

Ki passed the bow to Handstad. "Save it. Never is a long time."

"Not when it comes to oil fires, it ain't. 'Specially ones that aren't caused by some dumb mistake or spontaneous combustion," Handstad said.

"Then you suspect this one was set?" Ki asked.

"I don't know how yet, but it must've been done on purpose. From now on I'm posting guards and gonna fight fire with fire," Handstad said.

"Fight who?" Ki prodded.

"Cartinas."

"You sure Cartinas is behind it?"

"If you mean was they spied skulking about with a bomb, I reckon not. But tell me who else wants rid of us—you? Miss Starbuck? Ian, here? Nope, that tribe's been arguing for a fight, and by Satan's chandeliers, we'll cure them devils or break 'em."

"Okay, they're the only ones you know who've got motive. But just because of that, it's no more sensible to brand them guilty than it is for them to claim oilmen are responsible for rustling." Ki suddenly paused, caught by a thought, then frowned. "The hell it doesn't make sense," he said quietly, almost to himself.

Handstad blinked, perplexed. "What doesn't?"

"None of it does," Ferguson complained. "You've lost me."

"We're being baited into a war." Then, as though this were a full and sufficient explanation, Ki went on, "Listen, post your guards but hold off the fight. Talk it over with Teague first."

"The chief'll agree. He'll put the whammy on them."

"Ian, I'll meet you back at the ranch."

Scowling, Ferguson followed Ki to his horse, plainly hoping for more explanation. Ki was aware of that hope, but he first wanted to think hard and to poke into a few things. Before he talked further, he wanted to line out the situation as it actually existed and not as it was being cleverly made to appear.

★

Chapter 9

A Cartinas hand, one Ki had not seen before, was riding line along the boundary below the desert. He showed up at a gallop to intercept Ki, apparently having spotted Ki's approach from some distant vantage, but other than making a challenging gesture, he didn't attempt to stop Ki until Ki was within ten yards of the line.

"Veer off," he warned and drew his revolver. "This side is tight closed and I've got plain orders to shoot trespassers."

The man was flatly in earnest and Ki was aware that he would carry out his orders. Still, it was necessary to get by him.

"I'm crossing over to talk with your boss," Ki said, easing his horse almost to the line before halting. "I've got no feelings against you, but I won't talk Cartinas business with a hand, either."

The man shook his head. "Any closer and I'll empty your saddle."

Sighing acquiescently, Ki made a full, obvious turn

as though to swing his horse aside and back around. The man shifted his aim accordingly and relaxed a little, and as he did, Ki's turn became peculiarly hunched, then twisted. Then from his twisted position his *surushin*— his long rope belt with its two lead weights—snapped, whirling.

The man realized his mistake and tried to jerk his revolver back on target. In that instant, the spinning cord wrapped itself around his wrist, forearm, and upper torso, one of the lead balls smacking against his ribs. Unhorsed by the momentum, the man toppled, grunting, dropping his revolver. Ki, quitting his saddle in a flying leap, raced across to retrieve the revolver and pinion the stunned man before he could untangle himself.

The man was afraid, but put on a brave front. "You don't have to kill me, stranger. My foreman will when he finds out I goofed."

Ki smiled and began to unravel his belt. "Here's the deal. If you take my word that I'll go straight to Señora Cartinas and straight back out, you get your gun back and can go about your job. If not, you get to go in with me and explain how you wound up hog-tied."

The man stared stubbornly for a long moment. Finally the stubbornness gradually faded, and a small, sheepish grin quirked his lips. "I'll take it. Ain't often a guy can pull his neck out of a noose that easy. But if you raise hell or bear down on the *Señora*..."

Ki nodded and loosened the last of his belt. When they were both standing, he handed the revolver to the man and walked back to his horse, feeding his rope through the belt loops and slip-knotting the ends. Remounting, he nodded pleasantly to the man and rode on.

There were no further difficulties for the rest of the way in, but a ranch hand in the yard glimpsed Ki arriving and passed the word. Ev Moran and a flanking of men were waiting along the rail of the house veranda when Ki rode up. The crew looked as belligerent as before; Moran looked not merely hostile, but downright murderous.

"You got brass eggs, I'll own you that," Moran growled. "But your luck just ran out. And you're goin' out, flat out, feet first."

"You call it; I'll play it. But I came in peaceably."

"Like hell! You came up from the desert. I've had riders on that stretch day'n night, and you must've downed one to get past."

"He's still there in good shape." Ki leaned forward, crossing his hands on his saddle horn. "Look, Moran, I've got my own respect for the way you've backed Señora Cartinas against all comers, but you've got me and everybody else figured wrong, dead wrong."

"I doubt that!" Moran snapped. "You filching my wallet and suckering the sheriff is tally enough in my book. I ought've shot you the first time I saw you. Maybe I will—now."

Ki glanced at the flanking men, sensing the deadly tension building up, knowing his time was swiftly running thin. He tried his bid once more, no longer affable, his tone like the whetting of a sythe. "I'm through waltzing with you, Moran; I want to see Señora Cartinas. I told your line rider I don't talk business with a hand, and that goes for foremen, too, so climb off and go get her—"

The door behind Moran opened then, and Ysabelle came out onto the veranda. "All right, Ev," she said. "Start talking, Ki!"

Under this blunt invitation, Ki rapidly sketched what

118

had occurred at the well fire, ending with, "It was arson. The oilmen are convinced you somehow set it and are threatening retaliation."

"Whatever your reason for warning me, thanks. Let them come. We'll be prepared," Ysabelle replied sternly. "Let them put foot on my land, and they'll die in the desert in their putrid oil."

"You'd have heard of it anyway, I'm sure, in plenty of time to dig in and wait up along your line there. But what's south of here?"

"Nothing. Nothing but hills."

"And your big herd. Left virtually unguarded, while you pull most of your men and guns north to get ready against a rumored attack."

"Are you also warning of rustlers or stampeders?" Ysabelle gave a scoffing laugh. "Some threat. Our drive begins tomorrow."

"That leaves them tonight to grab your herd."

"They'd never get far," Moran interjected scornfully. "They'd have to head this way a fair piece before finding any canyon that'd land them west of the hills. After that, it's miles and miles of open country, and they couldn't make speed with such a herd. I tell you, no wideloopers would be so stupid as to try a strike like that."

"No, they're smart. They've planned ahead, undoubtedly spied on your gather and preparations, and've figured exactly when to hit for the fattest take. They'll outsmart you and drive to the south."

"What, across the San Joaquins?" Moran bellowed. "Why, the only half-assed route opens out above San Clemente, with no place to turn. It's miles 'pon miles around those hills, through lotsa sections where folks live. And where else could they take the herd?"

"To San Clemente."

"To—! What'n hell would they do with our cows there?"

"Sell them to the railroad."

Moran clamped his mouth shut. Ysabelle, too, stared at Ki as if firmly convinced that they were listening to a lunatic.

"Don't you see, Señora Cartinas?" Ki urged. "It's a natural. Except for the stock buyer, the railroad people don't know you, and even if they did, what would it matter? You'd not be riding with the herd; you've got to stay and care for your husband. You'd be sending your range boss, Moran, with credentials from you and authority to transact business. Is he known there? If someone else had your papers and claimed to be Moran, who would question it?"

"This's silly. Nobody else has any papers from me!"

"Oh, yes—a big, fat wallet full of them," Ki explained and turned to Moran. "I didn't steal your wallet, and no ordinary thief did either. It was one of the gang who knew just what they were after, and now they've got enough documents and your personal identification to deceive the railroad when they're presented."

Moran fidgeted, muttering, refusing to believe.

Ysabelle looked long at Ki. She stood erect and proud, the lamplight spilling from the windows emphasizing her anxious and determined features. A shame, Ki thought, and wished her life held more peace and tenderness and fewer problems which promised violence. At last she regarded Moran and asked him, "What do you think, Ev?"

Moran hunched his shoulders. "Señora, me'n the boys are with you till the last dog is hung. You know that.

But we ain't called on to believe every smooth-talking jackleg who wanders in here."

"True, but your wallet was stolen, and it did contain papers the bank wanted to see to grant me that loan. And there was the fire; we both saw the glow. If Ki is lying, he's gone to a lot of trouble to trick us," Ysabelle pointed out. "If he's right, we could be chasing around over west of the hills, while rustlers would be checking our herd in at San Clemente and collecting for it. Maybe the railroad would take the loss and pay again or give us back our cows. I wouldn't count on it; it's a whacking big amount of cash. I think we should take extra care tonight. How many are on guard now?"

"Three nighthawks. But confound it, *Señora!* Ki and the Starbuck crew and likely them oil gents will have everything you own going up in smoke in five minutes, if we tear off and left you here alone."

"I can protect myself and my husband, and the house is old. We can afford to rebuild it. We cannot afford to lose the herd." She stepped closer and touched Moran affectionately on the shoulder. "You and the crew have always stuck by me. Stick by now, Ev, please."

"Okay . . . And you, Ki, you're sticking by me."

Ki nodded, and Ysabelle smiled tautly. "Don't make it sound so threatening, Ev. Maybe we have found a neighbor we can trust, after all. I . . . I hope so."

Ki glanced at Ysabelle, but she had already turned and was stepping through the doorway into the house, her body moving provocatively, slender but softly rounded . . . quite a woman.

Grumbling "I can't spare men for bullshit like this," Moran compromised by selecting the seven already flanking him to take along. After they assembled with their weapons and mounts, he told them, "You heard the score. The *Señora* fears our herd might be rustled, so okay, we'll treat it seriously." He glared at Ki. "That way, when it proves a bust, this flimflammer won't have no excuses."

He signaled to follow and led them out of the yard in a southerly course. It was a tensely hushed ride, Moran silent and his men only occasionally talking in low voices, but never with Ki. And it was a wearisome ride with just a few short pauses to rest the horses as rolling plain became hardy upland and hills rose about interspersed with sloping meadows and valley pastures.

Eventually the hills seemed to melt away on both sides, and they walked their horses out past a contour which had cut off their view directly ahead. They drew up on a shelflike plateau overlooking a small pocket valley. Its floor was mostly the typical summer drypan, straw stubble, and a web of dry-wash gullies, but not far to their right was a low outcrop and a wide, shallow spring, around which sprouted bucknut, sage, and foot-high tufts of grass.

Blotching the valley were dark-shadowed batches of cattle, some lying down, chewing their cud, others up grazing. The murky outlines of horses were in a roped area at one end of the pool. At the other were hulking shapes of two canvas-topped wagons and the faint scarlet glow of a dying campfire. To the south, the sides of the valley rose, but a blacker section told Ki there must be a passage through. As of yet, however, he could not pick out any of the nighthawks who were supposedly minding the herd.

"I got saddlesored for nothin'," one of the men complained. "Them cows're all there and bedded so quiet they could be dead."

"Damn folderol," another agreed crossly. "Well, let's hie down there and settle in. Mayhaps Curly can brew us some coffee."

"Shut up," Moran ordered. "We're gonna act like Ki's phony rustlers exist, remember, so we can't let them hear or see us."

Dismounting, they began moving forward, keeping as low and noiseless as possible. Shadows were cast by the contours and by high brush growth along the ridged bank, and they made use of them as they stealthily led their horses on foot toward the camp. It took twenty minutes for them to reach the bushy fringe around the spring, and once inside its screening cover, Moran gestured for a halt.

Ahead, a man was sitting on a rock near the ember-smouldering fire. He was leaning on his rifle—a nighthawk taking his turn on duty. Through the grass and branches, Ki could see his slumped figure, and as he listened he heard the man cough.

"Stay put. I'll go forewarn him, so the rustlers lurking hereabouts don't see a big ballyhoo when we hit camp," Moran whispered. "C'mon, Ki, you're sticking by me, remember?"

Dropping his reins, Ki slipped with Moran around the edge of the spring and approached the nighthawk. They were almost to him when Moran snapped a twig, and the nighthawk whirled, rifle rising.

"Who's there?"

"Me, Brewster, Ev Moran. Keep it quiet."

Brewster walked over. "What's up?" he asked softly.

"Tell you in a minute. Where are Curly and Jack?"

"Sleeping," Brewster answered, pointing at the nearer of the two wagons, and then took Moran and Ki across to it. Crawling into the bed, he quickly roused the snoring nighthawks by shaking them.

"Pipe down," Moran warned, when Curly and Jack began groggily cursing Brewster. Tersely he explained why he and the others had come, sprinkling in a few profanities and colorful opinions. "Now, we're going to get set up, and we're going to do it right," he concluded. "I want Ki to have all the rope he needs to hang himself."

The other men were waved in. The wagons threw long black shadows that the dozen men utilized in stealing about, readying for a battle which eleven were convinced would never happen. Even Ki was starting to wonder if he had not been too hasty in suggesting it could; under sober reflection, the notion did appear preposterous and a mite daring for even the flintiest gang of owlhoots.

Shortly, they split into two teams. Six men fanned out across the valley floor to guard the herd, while the balance, including Ki and Moran, holed in around the campsite.

An hour passed . . .

Ki crouched beside a heavy wagon tongue on the west side of the encampment. Across from him was the waning fire, then the near end of the spring. Ahead and diagonally to his left was the broad, tapering mouth of the valley. Far to his right was the growing malignancy of the San Joaquins with their black gorges and pillars of weather-carved rocks. Behind was a lesser phalanx of jagged stone walls and side canyons, crooked and creviced, every one of them a spot for lurking ambush. They kept him straining his eyes their way . . . but it was while looking toward the valley mouth that he thought he first detected movement. Yet it was too distant and too dark to glimpse any detail. Then it was gone, leaving Ki with only an unpleasant premonition.

124

All remained calm...

It was eerie, waiting, holding still, keeping alert against a sneak attack without knowing if, much less when or from where, it would come. The tense night continued. No trouble. No strike. Ki felt pleased for Cartinas, but not with himself. He had been wrong...

Suddenly, from a dozen points, the night was laced with rifle fire. Beating swiftly from the direction of the valley mouth was a drumming of fast hoofs. Stunned by surprise, the Cartinas men rallied and answered with sparking guns. Another moment and a small horde of galloping riders streamed into the camp, their bullets clipping the wagon wheels or biting chunks of wood and canvas, though most slugs shrieked through the air to plug into the ground. They were met by a deafening salvo from the defenders, who were hidden under the wagons or in the concealing brush by the spring.

The riders rampaged through in a direct line for the herd, while two other groups, like wings, swerved in to join them from either side. The rope holding the Cartinas horses was broken, and the horses, frightened by the flashing shots, spooked and scattered. The cattle were milling, alarmed, churning around and bellowing, the portents of a stampede. From the overrun camp, six men went chasing futilely after the riders, shouting defiance, firing at will. Then the six detailed to guard the herd opened up, their heavy weapons roaring, flaming in the night, as they desperately tried stopping the yelling, shooting riders who were rushing the herd.

A few, then some, then all the cattle panicked. Heavy, blinded animals charged forward and nothing could halt their race. They broke through the thin lines, and the Cartinas crew scrambled out of their way, unable to check the stampede. Dust rose thick, and the thunder of hooves shook the earth.

The raiders pursued, their attention focused on running off as much of the herd as they could. Some of them caught up to ride point and veer the lumbering cows toward that black canyon in the southern face of the valley wall. Others swept alongside, acting as flank and swing, helping to block in the cows. Most of the force closed behind as drag, goading the laggards and stragglers, while fending off the Cartinas crew with their weapons blazing.

Ki could see the first cattle just moving into the narrow canyon mouth. The rustlers kept shouting, swinging rope goads, feeding the mass of frenzied beef through the hilly portals. None of the Cartinas men could prevent it, though they fought with a fury. Three rustlers spun from their saddles to lie without sound or motion, and Ki had counted at least two more who'd died back at the ruined campsite. A fifth yelled painfully as a bullet burned his ribs; he lurched, fell, and was trampled underhoof. Yet it was not without toll. Brewster, not far from Ki, threw up his hands and collapsed. Another ranch hand was crying out from a wound.

The crescendoing battle rang over the valley, but in the end, there was no saving of the herd. It flowed out of sight under a cloud of dust that glinted silver in the moonlight, the rustlers vanishing with it. The pounding of hooves dimmed, faded away . . .

★

Chapter 10

Left high and dry, the shocked, bloodied survivors tapered off their firing and stood watching in weary defeat. Then morosely they began hastening to do what had to be done. Weapons were checked and supplies were marshaled. The injured were tended; the two with major wounds were made comfortable as possible in a wagon with food and water at hand. The three who'd died were shrouded by the canvas top taken from the other wagon. Of the estimated two dozen rustlers, eight had fallen, but to Ki's disappointment, none had lived to talk. They were laid under the canvas, too. Finally the remaining seven men scoured the valley for their horses and regrouped back in camp.

Ki's eyes were coldly gray, his face bleak as the stone of the cliffs. Beside him, Moran was swearing lustily and shaking his fist toward the unseen rustlers. "Now let's light out after 'em!"

"They'll be on the lookout for us," Ki cautioned. "If we did catch up with them, chances are we'd just get ourselves gunned worse."

"Y'know, Ki, I guess the meanest chore a man ever has to do is 'fess to a whopping mistake. Well, I'm doing it. Accept my apology," Moran said and then declared vindictively, "But by God, I'm willing to risk anything to line my sights on those wideloopers. C'mon boys!"

He flung himself into the saddle and spurred down the valley. His crew, fired by his confidence, mounted and streaked after him. Ki went along, saying nothing, a furrow deep between his black brows.

From the start the canyon was narrow, with long and fairly steep banks. Then it began to squeeze in further, while it wound and twisted through the hills, following the tortuous course of some prehistoric river. It soon became evident to Ki that the rustlers riding point, flank, and swing would have been forced to drop back and join the drag, for there wouldn't have been room for them between the stolen herd and the encroaching, vertical cliffs.

Eventually they reached a section of the canyon which was shaped like a long, slender bottleneck with slopes consisting of a series of benches rising tier on tier to the distant skyline. A sharp bend distinctly marked the end of the sheer banks and the beginning of the slopes. They rounded the bend. Ahead was a straight stretch of nearly a mile, flanked on both sides by soaring benches. The lowest of these terraces, heavily overgrown with brush, was not much more than twenty feet above the level of the rocky, scrub-strewn floor.

As he had continually since entering the canyon, Ki surveyed the trail ahead and keenly searched the surrounding slopes. Abruptly his voice raised in a shout of warning. His words were drowned by a gunshot knifing the darkness, its powder flash winking from one of the benches. On its heels, flames lanced from three more spots, one from the same side and two from across on the opposing slope.

Curly, riding lead with Moran, wrenched halfway around and clutched his chest. Moran made a frantic sideward grab for him and missed, Curly slumping free and landing with arms flung wide, but the wild lunge undoubtedly saved Moran's life. A slug from the second volley sheared his hat brim and struck a ranch hand riding behind. The man toppled and was dragged by his plunging horse.

They had been caught in the apex of crossfire. The range was short, but dust, darkness, and their swift movement gave the others, more fortunate, a chance to escape. They swerved their mounts about and went racing for the protection of the curve, leaning low in their saddles, urging their horses to greater speed. Without further casualties they surged around the bend and wrenched their horses to a slithering, jostling halt. Weapons out and ready, they milled looking for targets. Our venturesome puncher, swearing revenge for the downing of his buddy, went back to the edge of the curve.

"Wait!" Ki yelled to him, just as the man peered around the edge—and got a bullet gouging the fleshy part of his arm as a reward for his daring. He retreated hastily, cursing viciously and wringing his blood-dripping fingers.

"They've got the bend covered," Ki said, "in easy range."

Moran was raving profanely. "What about my two boys they hit?" he demanded. "We've got to get back there and help them."

"From the way they dropped, I'm afraid they're beyond help," Ki replied grimly. "Anyway, we can't get to them. The rustlers left four behind to stall us, and four men holed up in those benches can hold against fifty coming around the bend."

"We can't let them stall us!" Moran raged. "There're five hundred in that herd, and I won't let them get away with it."

"They are getting away with it, straight to..." Ki paused thoughtfully. "If we had time to circle and jump them . . . Say, does the trail have anyplace like a waterhole where the herd might stop?"

"Nope. You drive it in one long push, right through."

"Well, is there another way to San Clemente?"

"Yeah, sorta, a path a few miles east of here. Runs south-southeast along the ridges and corkscrews. It's tough going, but horses can make it, though cows couldn't."

"Will it get us across before the herd?"

"Hmm . . . We could probably do it by dawn. I don't reckon the herd, even shoved damned hard, could make it before morning." His pugnacious face lit with a grin. "Ki, you done sold me. Just south of the trail's exit would be perfect. Those cattle can't move fast, and maybe we can catch 'em up before they have a chance to scatter. With luck, we'll bag the whole bunch."

Leading the way, Moran backtracked in search of a point where they could leave the trail and cut east. Finally he located what appeared to be a feasible route, and they sent their horses toiling up the steep slope. For a grueling hour they traversed through jagged rock and raking thorn, before intercepting the path.

The path over the hills proved to be as bad as Moran claimed, and worse. It was undoubtedly very ancient, but was now no more than a faint depression winding amid growth and over ledges, studded with boulders and washed out by rains.

"Nobody much used it 'cept Indians, prospectors, and hunters," Moran said. "Reckon nobody ever uses it now. In fact, only ol' scouts like me who grew up 'round here recollect it being here."

"That's all to the good," Ki responded. "Chances are the rustlers won't know about it either and'll figure so long as they hold the canyon trail, they're safe no matter what we decide to do. It might put them off guard and help us take them by surprise."

The rambling course southwest was hazardous to the extreme. The horses were often blowing hard by the time they reached the crest of rises, and it was necessary to call halts for a while to enable them to catch their wind. Frequently the descents were even more perilous, with broken necks being averted by what came close to miracles. The moon was low in the night sky now, and Ki became increasingly anxious. The ride was consuming much more time than Moran had anticipated. But to try hurrying it would be suicidal.

Moran was also growing worried. "It's about two miles before we dip down the flats—which ain't a'tall," he told Ki. "Then it's still a good ways to the trail's exit. I think we can make it, but we haven't time to waste. We've got to beat them there and find a place to burrow in, or all this riding will be for naught."

Soon the path plunged precipitously like a curlicue slide. Eventually the hills on either side began to fall away, and within another half hour, the coastal plateau ahead was visible. The sharp grades of San Joaquins continued to lessen, until they met and blended into the gradual slopes of the plateau. It was six. A cool, morning fog was drifting inland from the Pacific Ocean, not many miles away, and was diffusing the dawn. Grayness occupied the world.

Though no longer as steep, the path kept sinuously pitching and slewing downward as it skirted the San Joaquin's lower flanks. Shortly they could dimly see a gorge in the badland cliffs. From its bell-flared mouth, a churned-earth trail rolled south toward San Clemente, which was merely a misty shimmer of tiny lights and dull blots in the distance. Ki surveyed the skyline above the trail, but nowhere could he spy any telltale smudge of dust that would mark the passage of the Cartinas herd.

"The rustlers haven't cleared the hills yet," Ki remarked. "Looks like we can still be in time to catch them on the way out."

Heartened, they picked up their pace. Yet between them and the cattle trail was a lengthy slant of bank, shale and boulder-strewn, devoid of vegetation. The only practical route across was this rugged and winding track, which they rode at a reckless clip.

They were closing to within a half mile of the trail, when they glimpsed the van of the herd suddenly emerging from the gorge.

Moran swore profusely and sank steel to his horse. "Rifles!" he bellowed. "Shoot soon's they show, before they can spot us and scatter along the herd. It's our only chance to bag some of them."

The panting horses were sliding and skittering down the bank. Rocks rolled under them; gullies and crevices caused them to flounder. And the cattle were pouring from the gorge in a steady flow.

"A thousand yards," Ki murmured. "Long range for firing from horseback." With one hand he levered the carbine he'd borrowed yesterday and not yet returned. "Here goes 'cause here they come."

132

The last of the cows were through the mouth of the gorge. Behind them, in bunched formation, streamed the rustlers. Ki raised his carbine, his eye glancing along the sights. The others did the same. The plateau reverberated with the blast of gunfire.

The rustlers whirled, startled, in their saddles. Dazed with alarm, they ducked and dodged as lead stormed around them, and for a moment they seemed to hesitate, milling in wild confusion. Some tried to rally, clawing for weapons. But others, with slugs whining about their ears, were not slow to turn back and hunt for cover.

One rustler veered from the pack so fast that his hat got swept off. In that instant Ki recognized him, drew a swift bead, and shot. The rustler hurtled on for the safety of the gorge, untouched.

Urging his horse faster, Ki levered a fresh round while scanning for that man. It was difficult. More rustlers dashed for the gorge getting in his way, but Ki found him, sighted, and triggered. The man faltered, but rode on clinging to the mane of his horse and vanished in the swarm plunging into the gorge. The gang disintegrated into a panicky mob intent only on escape.

Yelling and swearing, the Cartinas riders charged down the slope with careless abandon, risking broken bones or death at every stride their horses made. Without accident they reached the trail, swerved toward the mouth of the gorge . . . but they didn't enter it.

They couldn't. The terrified cattle, bawling and milling, had floundered back until they choked the narrow mouth with a morass of rampaging flesh and bones. Try as they would, it was a good half hour before the sweating, cursing Cartinas men could get the entrance clear. And then they headed in after the rustlers.

"Hold it!" Ki shouted. "Hold it. It's no good. You're

doing the same thing you did back in the canyon. And the rustlers will do the same thing—hole up and blow us out from under our hats."

Moran considered and nodded. "Yeah, back off, boys. They got a break this time. Maybe it'll be different next time."

Grousing, the Cartinas hands complied. With savage looks and brandished fists, they turned their horses and filed out to begin regathering the herd. It had not scattered or even spread much, the cattle feeling little zest for moving after two stampedes and a long night's run. Which was good, because even with Moran and Ki helping hunt and gather strays, a five-puncher crew would have been no match against five hundred feisty critters. Soon the cows were again herded on the trail and trudging wearily southward.

Moran was exultant with relief, chortling over the recovery of the herd and congratulating Ki on his shrewd deductions. But Ki was in a bitter mood. He had hoped they would trap the rustlers, would kill or capture but in any case finish them. Instead, as Moran had said, they got a break. They escaped without a casualty.

Well, almost without a casualty. Ki knew he'd wounded that one man. His mood grew fouler as he recalled his first sight of the man's face, and his surprise at recognizing Whitey, Broderick Teague's thug of a receptionist, his murky eyes flaming, and his thatch of tow hair like a pale yellow beacon when his hat fell off.

Because the California Southern Railroad had decided to expand its facilities here for its push north, San Clemente had assumed added importance, becoming a thriving town overnight. Offices and stores and hotels crowded the sidewalks, while on lanes and open tracts shanties and adobes huddled in haphazard arrangements. There was a saloon every square yard it seemed—saloons in tents and saloons in more elaborate quarters. People thronged the streets and, as the herd jostled and bleated past, they shouted questions about the shooting they'd heard. But the Cartinas crew rode on, shaking their heads.

Just south of town, the expansive train yards were in a ferment. Lining the welter of shiny, newly laid rails were locomotives, freight cars, and coaches being worked on. Trackside were great stacks of supplies and equipment, loading platforms, sheds and shops galore, with frames of new buildings awaiting completion. Laborers, trainmen, surveyors, and construction engineers bustled about despite the early hour. But without undue delay, Moran received direction to where stockmen were prepared to receive his herd, tally the cows, and shunt them into pens.

Ki left Moran there and went to a nearby workman's cafe for a hearty breakfast. He was about to go when Moran entered.

"Good news and bad news," Moran said, joining him. "Good news is the railroad's paying off to me after the tally, no questions."

"That *is* good news."

"Well, there was a question at first. But I told what happened and showed 'em the brands on our horses. Then the stock buyer came and made me describe the ranch interior—he remembers it from his visit there—and I convinced him I was the me who lives there."

Ki had to chuckle. "All right, what's the bad news?"

"The tally's gonna take awhile. If that ain't enough, my story got the police chief called in, and now I gotta fill out reports on the rustling and my wallet and such and stick around while he investigates I dunno what. Ain't nothing up at the gorge."

"Sounds like you're going to be tied up here."

"All day. Now, this don't have to hold you up. But if you're going back, I'd sure appreciate it if you'd detour by the ranch and tell the *Señora* that I'll be late and everything's fine."

Ki grinned. "Sure, Ev, glad to. It won't be out of my way. I'm taking the path anyway on the chance the rustlers will hole up on the trail, hoping to lift your poke and willing to settle for me."

Moran matched his grin. "No, I reckon they don't care much for you, Ki. It would've been a lot different for them—and us—if you hadn't bulled in when you did. I'm beholden to you, I am."

"You're liable to be asked to honor that debt before long," Ki replied enigmatically, "and to help collect a few overdue ones."

Moran frowned quizzically, but Ki did not see fit to elaborate further right then. The time would come, though; it was fast approaching.

Chapter 11

Ki bought a horse.

He had no choice. The hostler at the livery stable wouldn't rent him one, irascibly reminding Ki that Vinada was not a drop-off point for San Clemente nags. And the horse he'd been riding, the chestnut gelding Teague had loaned him, had been used long and rested short these past couple of days and was tuckered to a frazzle. So Ki boarded the chestnut, Moran promising to take it back with his bunch later, and then dickered with the hostler over a deep-brisketed mare. Pocketing the bill of sale and a receipt to give Jessie for her expense records, Ki switched gear and headed north.

The mare proved sturdy and well disposed. It followed the path diligently without needing to be urged, and Ki unintentionally napped asaddle much of the way. Back in the small valley he found the wagons and wounded gone and some fresh graves, indicating this part of the news he had to report was already known.

He arrived at the ranch soon after dark.

A light was shining through the salon window, and there were sounds of a blacksmith hammering in one of the barns, but Ki saw no one when he pulled up to the veranda. He dismounted and was loosening the cinch when another light flared in a wing of the residence. He watched its progress and the salon brighten. Then the door opened and Ysabelle stepped out holding a lamp. She was wearing an embroidered kimono, belted at the waist, and her form was softly outlined beneath the clinging robe.

"Just you?" she asked in dismay. "But where are . . . ?"

"Safe," Ki replied and relayed the news.

"Thank goodness." She eased with relief. "Put your horse away while I fix you something. You both look hungry."

Ki couldn't deny that. He led the mare across to the barn, where the blacksmith helped provide it a rubdown, feed, and a stall. Ysabelle came to meet Ki as he returned and ushered him through to a small, informal dining area off the kitchen. Its round clawfoot table was set with cold chicken, side dishes, and a decanter of wine.

"Leftovers from supper," she said, pouring the wine. "I'm afraid the cook's off for the night, and my housekeeper's ill."

"Looks delicious." It was and after the meal Ki rested to let it digest. He was glad of the respite, for he knew there was still much to be done as speedily as possible. Ysabelle took the plates into the kitchen, and when she returned to sit down again, Ki noticed a glitter of tears welling in her eyes.

"What's the matter?" he asked gently.

"I . . . I've had a pretty rough day," she faltered. "When my hands checked on the herd this morning, and I learned of the fight, the dead and injured, the rustling . . . Well, my heart plummeted. And then this afternoon, when Ian Ferguson and his crew barged in here looking for you, I felt as though I was facing some hostile enemy."

"I see. Did they leave as friends or foes?"

She daubed her eyes. "I'll tell you what I told them, Ki. When the prodding's done and we can work stock and nothing else, we will be easy open to them and all neighbors. Not until."

She was fudging, Ki sensed. In her heart, she was eager for warmer ties. But he also knew she was afraid, her abiding love for Cartinas not allowing her to accept friendship for fear a softness within herself would betray the land she was struggling to retain.

Defiantly she added, "Don't think I cry over it, Ki."

"Everyone has a right to let their hair down now and then."

"Not me. I won't buckle," she replied in her old brash tone. She fell silent, glancing at him and then at her hands clasped in her lap. "You mix me up," she murmured and lapsed silent again.

He sat there, unresponsive. He didn't wish to argue with her; he was still fatigued and too logy from food and wine to fight.

Suddenly, with complete unexpectedness, Ysabelle said in a choked up voice, "Damn you! Oh, damn you anyway!"

He straightened. "Now what's the matter?"

"I'll tell you what's the matter. I . . . You . . ." And then she was weeping, hysterically, without restraint or control.

For several moments she wept alone. Then Ki rose

and went to her, placing his arms comfortingly on her shoulders as she slumped in her chair. Her weeping continued, as though there was a intolerable burden inside her which had to be released. Ki tilted her head back and with his napkin tenderly wiped away her tears.

"It's been so long, so long," she said.

She drew to her feet, her hand coming around and pressing the back of his neck. She stood tight against him and her face was pale under the cloud of her hair. She was hot, Ki realized; there was a fire deep within her of frustrated yearning, and despite his best intentions, he sensed an answering fire igniting in him. When a woman gets wanting, a man gets willing, and Ki no longer felt tired at all.

"Ramon can't now," she sobbed against his chest. "He never could much before. Anyway, I love *the* Cartinas, not *a* Cartinas . . ."

Her lips found his, lightly at first, but with a demanding passion that increased and would not be denied. Not that Ki wished to deny it. He couldn't help reacting to the unrequited hunger rising through her body, and his own lips were as hungry, as eager as hers. They embraced almost savagely, the fires mounting in them.

Slowly, then, while keeping pressed against Ki, Ysabelle eased down to sit in her chair again, her hands gliding along his chest and abdomen and thighs. Her curious fingers found the bulge of his growing erection and traveled its length, and she made a whimpering sound in her throat as she traced his thickening column, while her other hand nimbly untied his rope belt and unbuttoned his fly. Hurriedly she tugged his jeans down and grasped his exposed shaft.

"Ahh, *estupendo* . . ." She licked her lips.

Ki rubbed a hand through her hair. "Your kimono . . ."

140

She shook her head, bent closer. Her eyes closed and her full-lipped mouth opened, and her pink tongue fluted out to lick the crown of his manhood. She seemed to taste him, to see if she liked it, then she fitted her mouth over to swallow him whole.

Her teeth scraped along his aching girth as she tightened her lips and began a tentative sucking motion. Her hands stroked his buttocks and cupped his scrotum, gently squeezing, while she bobbed her mouth back and forth. Ki gasped and watched, his eyes flaring as she sucked harder and absorbed more of his flesh into her clasping mouth, his hips beginning to move in concert, his groin boiling, threatening to spill over. Ki fought to hold back, the sensations feeling exquisite, because she acted so hungry about it . . . until without warning, she released him and lifted her head.

"First the hors d'oeuvre, now the entree," she said, smiling.

Sensuously she stood up and turned her back to him, hiking her robe up and tucking it around her waist, baring herself from her feet to her taut, rounded bottom. Leaning back on the table, she positioned herself with her head cradled on one arm.

"Come," she cooed. "Come."

Ki moved closer and ran his hands across her naked cheeks and between her inner thighs touching a finger to her, feeling the moisture of her anticipation. She moaned, contracting rhythmically with his touch.

But when he tried to loosen her robe, she said, "Don't."

"I'd like to see you completely naked."

"I know. It's better when you're naked, but someone might come along; you can never tell." Feeling Ki pressing against her she arched to reach and clasp his hardness, guiding it to her warm sheath. "You stay dressed, too."

141

Ki slid inside her a long way before he realized how tight she was. He paused and looked down at her trembling hunched figure.

"*Más, más...*" she urged breathlessly. "More, more..."

He lanced deeper into her again, and this time he could almost feel the very depth of her. He began to pump hard then, and she seemed to grow even tighter around him, until every time he would thrust into her, she would gasp, shuddering, from the impact. Yet she kept begging while undulating her buttocks back against him, greedy for more. There was nothing timid or gentle about this union, Ki thought, as he plunged to the hilt in her gripping hot depths.

Her thighs pistoned in tempo with his strokes, and her inner muscles clasped him as if she would hold him forever. Her gasps became moans, soulful and prolonged, and she sunk her mouth into her arm in an attempt to keep from screaming in a cascade of incoherent emotion. She was consumed by the fire in her that was mounting like a holocaust, devouring everything but the hunger to have Ki go on, to have him finish what she had begun.

"Hurry," she whimpered.

Her pleading choked off in a staccato sputtering as she shuddered convulsively in orgasm. Ki, yielding to his own burgeoning climax, speared forward simultaneously, embedding and ejaculating deep inside her.

They collapsed in a satiated heap, Ysabelle sprawling on the table beneath Ki's spent form. For a while they stayed pinned that way, savoring the fulfillment of their pressing need. When at last Ki withdrew from her, Ysabelle straightened on wobbly legs, throbbing with a peculiarly satisfying ache, though it was becoming tempered by an aftermath of guilt and self-incrimination.

"There's something about you that makes people do what they never figured to do," she said with a sigh, turning and smoothing her kimono back down. "Don't worry. I blame myself, not you."

"It was nobody's fault. It happened, is all."

"Is that all you can say about it?"

"What do you want me to say?" he asked mildly.

"Tell me I'm too decent, too respectable to seduce you and cuckold my husband. Tell me I'll pay for my sins, that I'll rot in hell for my selfishness, for my wantonness. Rake me good, Ki."

"I won't, because I don't believe any of it," Ki said firmly. "You are a fine lady, Ysabelle, and that's my considered opinion."

She looked disgusted. "Just goes to show you don't know much about women."

"That's something I've never claimed," Ki replied with a laugh, checking to be sure he was properly buttoned and belted. "Stop whipping yourself. I do know that passion and desire don't make anyone feel sick or guilty. Only the hate and resentment that can be hidden in them will cause sickness and bitter regrets."

She smiled, first tentatively, then fully, and leaned against his chest. "I don't know about that, but you make me feel better."

"Good. Now much as I want to stay, I really must go."

"Will I see you again?"

Soberly Ki said, "Perhaps sooner than you think . . ."

Chapter 12

Soon Ki was climbing stiffly into the saddle again and trotting his horse out of the yard. Instead of cutting north, he stayed on the ranch's wagon road, which common sense and the blacksmith said would take him to Vinada.

The mare pranced, chomping at the bit, high-spirited after its feed and rest, and Ki, similarily impatient, let it have head. Nosing out, mane flying, tail streaming behind, it stretched into an impetuous run. Ki settled to the hull, thinking about the Cartinas woman and wondering about the two yet to be visited. He still kept a vigilant eye on the passing terrain. It was good range and would make money once the ranch was again on its feet, but it was dark range, the moon just showing itself through shredded clouds—which according to Ki's calculations would make it about nine o'clock. And the horse just kept on burning the trail, showing no signs of wanting to quit.

144

At one point a roving Cartinas sentry sang out a challenge, and Ki slowed to make himself known. Then he allowed his horse to race on, his senses remaining tuned to a keen pitch. But there were no further interruptions, and the mare was scarcely beginning to flag when finally they reached the outskirts of town.

Ki forced the gait down, fighting for the bits and reins, and circled about to approach the offside of Broderick Teague's grand home. He passed through rear lanes and back fields until he came to a long, narrow thicket that bordered the property. Low and scrubby, the hedge offered poor concealment, but it was the best to be had, so Ki jogged along it to where the growth appeared densest.

Ground-reining his horse, he paused, listening warily. He heard only its breathing, which wasn't even blowing—the fool steed seemed as fresh as a horse just out of a stable! Then swiftly yet cautiously, Ki moved through the entangling brush and emerged onto the grounds roughly parallel with the stable. Checking to make sure nobody was about, he sprinted across the open space and ducked around the side of the house. He reached a short flagstone porch with a couple of steps. He listened sharply at a door then tried its handle, gratified to find the door wasn't locked. He slipped inside and stood in a dark pantryway, ears acute, trying to recall what he knew of the plan of the house.

From the doorway on his left, through which was the kitchen, came the clatter of dishes and the humming of one of the maids. On his right, however, where a corridor led to the dining room, all was perfectly still. Ki edged along the corridor, carefully alert against being surprised by the maid or anyone else, and crossed the dining room to a set of doors. Inching them apart, he squeezed by into the foyer of a parlor. On the far side of the room, he recognized the entryway and wide door that led to the porte-cochere, while opposite him was the stubby hallway to Teague's business offices. Midway between was the staircase to the second floor bedrooms.

Ki went up the stairs, keeping close to the wall so that the treads wouldn't creak. Moving like a drifting shadow, he headed from the landing to the guest quarters where, he remembered, Jessie was supposed to have been installed, next door to Alice's room.

Pausing with his fingers on the door knob, Ki failed to hear anything through the thick, solid panel. He knocked guardedly, then opened the door enough to slip in, shutting it quickly behind him.

"So there you are!" Jessie's voice was loud, sharp, and expectant. Her stance matched her words. She stood stiffly by her bed across the room. Ki raised a finger to his lips in a quieting gesture, but she ignored it, declaring in the same dramatic tone, "I saw you sneaking across the grounds through the window, and don't you dare try to deny it."

"Sneaking across the grounds through the window," Ki mocked softly, starting toward her, not yet understanding the game but figuring he should play along. "How'd I manage that neat trick?"

"Always full of smart sass, aren't you, you savage!"

She sounded almost sincere, except that Ki saw a glint of humor instead of malice in her eyes. Then he glimpsed a piece of paper in her hands, with which she was making slight, furtive signs to attract his attention. Going to the window, he took the paper from Jessie as he brushed past, while she continued berating him.

"Oriental savage, that's what Broderick called you.

He was just here minutes ago, telling me about your loathsome behavior!"

For a moment Ki gave no answer, apparently peering out the window. But it was Jessie's note which had his attention.

> *Teague is hiding in the closet. He saw you from the window. Shall we lead him on? What is going on, anyhow?*

Teague's presence and vilifying denunciations indicated to Ki that Whitey had contacted him since the gunfray at the gorge. And, therefore, it was evident that Teague was in league with the rustlers and was liable to have a few such thugs nearby to back his hand. So, although Ki had come to get Jessie and Alice, wanting to get them clear before they could be menaced, he realized that to force a showdown here and now would likely endanger them even worse. He decided it best to pretend to abandon Jessie. Once Teague left, he could slip back and the three of them could do a vanishing act.

Turning, he noted the closet door was ajar. Winking while saying "I imagine you'll throw another tantrum now," he crossed to lean against the door, closing it firmly. "I only wish your tiny pal was still here. I'd ask him if he told you about sending his oaf of an office boy to help rustle the Cartinas herd last night."

"I don't believe you!" Jessie affected enough contempt to mask her concern and questioning look. "Broderick would never do that!"

"Did he tell you how he had Ev Moran's wallet snatched?" Ki persisted. "Or how he's been stealing your ranch blind? Or having Ramon Cartinas ambushed and

Ysabelle branded as a crooked bitch?"

"No, he told me of your bar brawls and scrapes with the law, and of being suspected of torching his oil well," Jessie retorted, though clearly growing more bewildered the more she heard. "You're despicable, smearing lies against a wonderful man like Broderick!"

"The pipsqueak won't keep his hero halo on for long, Jessie. He's too tight to board you here if there's nothing in it for him."

"Why, how dare you! Just because your only interests are in wenching trollops and leeching off my money, don't think that's all another man would see in me. I'll have you know Broderick has sworn his undying love and has asked me to marry him." She made a quick face at Ki in response to the flash of surprise on his face.

"Shorty must be a fast worker," Ki said scoffingly. "Well, I just came to get you, not wed you. Are you coming with me?"

"Leave the company of a *gentleman* to go off God knows where with a brazen ruffian?" Jessie exclaimed. "I should say not!"

"Suit yourself." Shrugging, Ki straightened from the closet and went to open the hall door. Pausing on the threshold, he glanced back to add, "I'll try to stick around somewhere for the wedding, so I can send my compliments and a present. I'll send a stool, so the shrimp will have something to climb on when he wants to kiss you."

Jessie clapped a hand over her mouth, not quite knowing whether to appear outraged or to repress a laugh. And then without a sound the hall door closed and Ki was gone.

But not far. Across the hall Ki spied the narrow door of a linen closet. He stepped into it quickly and drew the door almost shut, holding it with the tip of one of his daggers, for there was no inside knob to release the latch if it were completely closed.

He was none too soon, either. For a moment later the door of Jessie's room burst open, and Teague rushed out fuming with indignation and injured pride. He hesitated, addressing Jessie reassuringly, "Don't fret, m'dear. I'll see that scoundrel doesn't get away with his snide insinuations. Shrimp! Pipsqueak, he called me! I'll—You just make yourself easy and don't worry your dear head."

With that, Teague hastened away and down the stairs. Ki waited a good minute and was on the verge of stepping out and returning to Jessie's room, when he caught footsteps coming up the stairs. A maid appeared carrying a tray. She approached Jessie's door, knocked, and went in. "I've fetched you this warm milk to help you sleep," Ki heard her say. "There's a dollop of brandy in it, too. 'Night."

Ki watched as the maid reappeared and closed the door behind her. She paused thoughtfully and then, to his alarm, moved toward the linen closet, her hand reaching for the knob. Ki levered his dagger to wedge the door against her pull, fearing that a hard pull on the door would snap the high-tempered steel of his thin blade.

Ki felt her first sharp tug on the knob, heard her mumbling with disgust at the door's stubbornness. There were several more sharp tugs, and he knew a satisfaction at the ability of his knife to meet the situation. The maid took a pace back, as if to regard the offending door, then turned and seemed to be on her way. Ki followed the sound of her steps—which halted abruptly, dashing his hopes. He heard her raised voice as she called out, "Hilda? Hilda, come up here and help me open this broom closet, will you? I want a dust rag, but it's tight shut."

Two hefty matrons ganging up on the door could

probably rip it clean off its hinges. Preferring not to be flat discovered in hiding, Ki stepped out swiftly, silently, shutting the door and taking a backward step. Thus, he hoped to appear to have just come along the hall when the maid glanced back at the balky door.

"May I help?" Ki offered and easily opened the door. But his pleasantness and accommodation aroused no confidence in the maid's startled bosom. "Lordy!" she gasped, sucking in her breath. "Lordy!" Her feet took wing and she flew for the stairs.

Wasting no time cursing the luck, Ki dodged into Jessie's room. She sprang out of her chair where she'd been sipping the milk, almost dropping the glass from the sudden, unexpected sight of him.

"We've got to get out of here, fast," Ki said in a clipped, low tone. "I ducked into a linen closet across the hall to wait till Teague left, and the maid had to want in to get a dust rag."

"What *is* happening, Ki?" Jessie demanded. "What's all your crazy talk about Broderick having a herd rustled and swiping a wallet and stealing my cattle and plotting against the Cartinases and all?"

"I know 'em all for a fact, except him being responsible," Ki said hastily. "I'm quite sure he is, and I tossed that in just to give him something else to chew on awhile. I don't know why or how the deal fits together. I do know we have to get Alice and scram."

"Well, I don't know why we have to go now," Jessie complained, "but I'll trust you have a reason. And for blaming Broderick, too."

Easing into the hall, they glided the short length to Alice's room and stealthily entered. Alice was sleeping placidly, her face having the pallor of one who'd come through a bad time and had lost some blood, but who was no longer critically hurt. She awakened at their steps, light as they were, and sat up awkwardly with a bleary smile of curiosity and welcome on her face. "S'nice to see—"

Jessie shushed her. "We're leaving. Don't ask; just do."

Unhesitatingly, seeming to accept the order on faith, Alice shucked back the covers. Wearing only a flowing Empire-style nightgown of pink nainsook, she swung her feet to the floor. "Hand me my clothes and boots," she whispered, "and please turn your backs."

"Listen, there isn't time," Ki said softly yet urgently. "We have to get out of this place quickly; do you understand?"

Alice, nodding, weaved unsteadily toward the door and crashed into the dresser. Ki caught the wash bowl as it fell off, then grasped Alice before she fell too, as he put the wash bowl back. Holding her upright, he headed out to the hall. Jessie, taking the girl's boots along, quietly closed the door after them.

Breathlessly they crept to the landing and down the stairs, fearing their footfalls might be audible. They could hear the other maid calling, "Grace? Grace, what is the nonsense now?"

They padded across the foyer to the entrance door, Ki half supporting, half dragging Alice in his haste. Then they were outside, where Alice sat for a moment to pull on her boots. The night air seemed to strengthen her, and after her assurance that she was fine on her feet now, they hurried in along the thick shadows that lined the drive from the porte-cochere to the stable at the rear.

Ki was hoping Teague had left the house before the maid's alarm was spread, but he wasn't counting on it. They needed transportation or concealment, and the stable offered possibilities. Heading for it, he noticed lamplight glowing from within. Glancing at Alice, he realized she simply wouldn't pass muster, so when they had almost reached there, he called a halt.

He asked Alice, "How're you feeling?"

"Weak but willing," she gamely answered.

"All right, see that hedge?" Ki pointed toward the spot he'd come through earlier. "Just on the other side, you'll find my horse. Take it up to the street in front. We'll meet you there."

"Why . . . ?" Looking from the hedge to her gown, Alice smirked. "Ah yes, what would the good stable hands think if they saw this?"

"Just do some tall praying no one sees you," Ki said, as she started hastening across the grounds. "Or much of us, either."

Watching to make sure of her progress, Jessie and Ki waited with mounting tension, aware that minutes could mean the difference between clean escape and failure. Soon as Alice vanished into the hedge, they turned to sprint toward the stable, gambling that the hostler there wouldn't yet know of the situation.

They strode confidently inside, and Jessie flashed the hostler a cheery smile. "Sorry to bother you, but Broderick said you could stake me and Ki to another pair of good fast saddlers," she announced.

The hostler squinted at Ki. "Where's your last one?"

"Lounging fat at Ferguson's ranch," Ki lied heartily.

"Uh-huh. Well, no more comin' back without your horse, y'hear, or worse, your horse comin' back without you. Like *she* done."

"Sure, we'll return us and them together," Ki promised, glancing to where the grouchy hostler was thumbing. The *she* referred to was a piebald mare in a nearby stall, and Ki recognized it even before he walked a pace to get a clear look. "The horse belongs here, eh?"

"Yep. John Smith's favorite, she is, and how she wandered in alone in a dang mystery to me. The boss is mighty upset, too." The hostler spat and started away. "I'll have you saddled in a jiffy."

Jessie had been eyeing the mare wonderingly, and when the hostler was out of earshot, she murmured, "That's Billy the Buck's."

Ki nodded. "Or John Smith's, depending if you prefer aliases. In any case, that's the horse we turned loose to bring its empty saddle home. This is home. You heard what the hostler said."

"You mean Broderick hired—"

"Later," he cut in urgently, as the hostler led the first horse from a stall. Jessie mounted and sat with stymied perplexity. Moments later the second horse was ready, and Ki swung aboard.

Thanking the hostler, they left for the lane. As Ki had discovered earlier, the only real way to ride on or off the grounds was via the house and street out front. They had no idea what to expect, how many men Teague might have around the place, or what kind of uproar would result if they were detected. So they chose to take a quiet gait that would be less likely to attract attention.

Nerves screwed tight, they ducked under the porte-cochere and traversed the rest of the lane to the street. Turning, they walked along it to just past the edge of the property, where they located Alice some yards back in the shadows, waiting anxiously afoot beside the mare. Dismounting, Ki motioned her forward and helped boost her up on the horse he'd just been loaned, and though he tried to maintain an outward calm and easy smile, tension throbbed within him while he took time to adjust the stirrups to her shorter legs.

Ki was settling on his horse when the front door of the house tore open and Teague sprang out on the pillared porch. His voice was savagely castigating, and the hulking figure of a man followed him—a tow-headed man with his arm in a sling.

They didn't wait to be spotted. They were still too close and exposed to escape detection once Teague's eyes bore their way, and they preferred to be on the fly when that occurred. "Keep your horse moving, whatever else," Ki called to Alice. With lashing reins and goading flanks, they sent their mounts into a hard run. Wheeling, they galloped together down the street toward the edge of town.

"It's them! It's him!" Teague raged behind them. And then sounded the pungent discharge of a gun, an orange tongue of flame flicking out into the night, and the snarl of hot lead passed nearby. "Stop it, you dummy! You might hit the women! Get the saddlers!"

Another moment and they were well clear of the house. They slowed somewhat so as not to break the horses, and Jessie raised her insistent voice again. "Ki, I want to know precisely what's—"

But again her question did not get finished, did not receive an answer. For Ki caught the sudden hammer of hard-pounding hooves from somewhere not far behind. He jumped his mare sideward, grabbing Alice's horse by the bit to keep from losing her, and with Jessie following, plunged into the blackness of a narrow alleyway between two buildings. There they pulled up, waiting.

Less than a minute later three horsemen raced by.

"Fast workers," Ki murmured, as the hoofbeats receded in the distance. He nudged his horse moving again and brought them out to the rear alley behind the buildings. He turned to Alice. "You're more familiar with the town. Which way now?"

Guided by Alice, they swiftly threaded among clustered hovels and through odd back sections of deepest darkness. At last they cleared Vinada proper, but rode unceasingly onward until well onto Jessie's rangeland. Then cutting from the wagon road to a spindly wedge of trees; they reined in to allow their horses a breather.

This time Jessie was adamant. "Okay, Ki, spill. I'm utterly confused by it all, and I'd admire hearing right now what's going on and what makes you so sure any of it is Broderick's work."

Ki stretched, sighed, and launched into a detailed account of all that had transpired. "There's a pattern," he said, summing up. "It isn't only a rustling gang, or only a few random ambushes, or only a coincidental this or that. Sure, there're lots of unknown loose ends, but what is known smacks of a coordinated scheme for some reason, planned by someone with brains to run it and money to invest in it. I might've suspected the man I overheard at the hotel, but he spoke of a boss, so he's just a lieutenant. Whitey couldn't control such an operation; he hasn't the smarts of Billy the Buck's horse, but he and the horse both returned to their roost, didn't they? And none of this was happening before Teague arrived, right? And who else could it be? Yes, I think Teague is the spider in the middle of the web."

Jessie looked shaken, almost stunned.

Alice gasped, "So it must've been his men who knifed me! And then for him to take me in . . . !" She sucked in an angry breath. "He took me in, all right, took us all in. Oh, that double-dealing dog!"

"I can't believe it," Jessie cried. "Father trusted him—"

"Your father judged people for what they were at the time, not what they'd been a month, a year, or a decade before," Ki reminded her gently. "Judge Teague for yourself, for what he's now."

"Yes . . . Yes, I should; I will. You're right, Ki."

"Maybe not. I don't know all the kinks in this snake track and maybe I'm condemning him too soon. When a man uses fists or a gun or his brains, I can see a fight is fair and'll take him on his own odds. But when I judge he's using treachery, deceit, women—"

"Señora Cartinas the worst of all," Alice broke in. "It's pure lies he spread about her, about them running burned brands, isn't it?"

Ki chuckled. "Ysabelle is true as a die. The Cartinas tribe has been wild, but that's all, and she's much the same. I suspect the lies, along with the rustling and poisoning and so forth, have been to stoke a range war between us and Cartinas."

Then they continued on. The moon, having emerged from behind the clouds, dappled the terrain with light, and Jessie rode and surveyed the opaqued hills while thinking carefully of Broderick Teague. On reflection she found that his genteel, ingratiating manner, which at first had assured and convinced her so strongly, seemed increasingly affected and insincere. Came the dawning, and now some of the other puzzling pieces began falling into place.

Shortly, the wagon road was bordering the rim of the desert, and they came to the fork where the short cut led down through the oil field. They didn't take the trail this time, of course, preferring to stay on the longer yet safer road to the ranch.

Nonetheless, as Jessie gazed toward the yonder field, she felt reasonably certain that the vast majority, if not

156

all, of the oil workers were innocent. They were simply too professional, too dedicated, too foreign to range life to be involved. The menial laborers and those just hanging around could be a different matter, but they'd be few—the regular crew would see to that—which meant Teague must keep his gang stashed in the hills or someplace, hidden ready to spring out and snap up without warning. Well, lately his traps hadn't been tripping quite right. Now it was up to her, Jessie decided, to set one up for him that wouldn't miss. Already an idea was forming, and as she rode, she mulled over details.

The ranch was dark and silent when they arrived.

But not for long. After stabling their horses, they quietly entered the house. Ferguson awoke anyway and staggered from his bedroom, wearing a striped nightshirt and brandishing a candle. He let out a joyous whoop, which got Bertha up, and she shuffled in. Greetings were exchanged, questions were fielded, lamps were lit. Bertha promptly declared a hot meal was in order and assaulted the kitchen with a frenzy. The unusual activity rousted the daycrew from their snoring in the bunkhouse, and within minutes High-pocket loped inside, barefooted and barechested, hitching his jeans and demanding to know what the middle-of-the-night crisis was about.

They all retired to the kitchen table. The commotion seemed to have promoted appetites, and they almost managed to lay waste to Bertha's mountainous platters and bottomless coffee pot. Conversation centered on a single topic, a frustrating one. For despite the continual probing, Jessie remained politely evasive, just as she'd been since they'd arrived. Ki and Alice were too, once they'd caught on. This was Jessie's subject alone; it was her prerogative when and how to broach it.

Jessie stalled until the meal was through. Ferguson

went for a cigar, lighting it when he sat down again. Then along with High-pocket, who had tilted his chair on its back legs, Ferguson watched Jessie grow serious and lean forward to speak.

Jessie outlined the general situation as she saw it. She did not present a precise plan; it was still tentative and could be given them later. Now was the time to explain where Starbuck stood and why and to let these men, and through them the crew, choose once more whether to stick or drift. She wished she could postpone it. Prospects of peace were rapidly diminishing hereabouts.

They listened quietly, attentively. When Jessie finished, High-pocket righted his chair and padded to the stove for more coffee. Ferguson chewed on his cigar, his rugged face twisted wryly. When High-pocket returned, he looked sternly at Ferguson. "Well?"

"Well, what?"

"Well, we do it."

"Outmanned and outgunned?"

"Higher the hog, the harder the fall." High-pocket sat down, scowling. "I can stomach a louse who steals for himself. But one who'd steal and kill for hire, get neighbors feuding, drygulch a gent and pick the wife for his goat, who'd stab your kid—!"

Jessie smiled inwardly. High-pocket had delivered his decision before knowing Ferguson's own position. In fact, he'd been arguing for a showdown, and the devil with his boss's intentions.

And Ferguson chuckled, viciously, low in his throat. "That's sweet to hear from you, High-pocket, 'cause I'd have gone done it alone. Tell the boys straight, now, but tell 'em we *will* do it—without the law, 'twixt Satan and the high blue butte, all by ourselves!"

"Maybe not, Ian," Jessie said. "Come daylight, a few

158

hours sleep, and some fresh horses, Ki and I will go out recruiting."

"To Vinada?" Ferguson shook his head. "Jessie, Teague will have snapped up every son of a horn toad in town by now."

"To Cartinas."

"Thunderation! That'd be like trying to draw honey from a hornet's nest. It ain't there for the askin'."

Ki shrugged. "They've got strong reason to side us."

"And a chili-fire queen who roasted us to a crisp when we was there yesterday askin' about you." Ferguson bit deeply into his cigar. "T'hell with 'em. All I'm after is to get in close enough to tag Teague men with every round in the chamber of my gun."

High-pocket grinned faintly. "I'll bet you a new saddle I get two scalps for every one you do, Boss," he challenged.

It was an attempt at humor, but it hid nothing. Jessie knew she was probably taking her crew out to die and the knowledge didn't set easy. She was also exhausted and soon excused herself to retire; the others agreeing it was late rose from the table with her.

Sleep proved elusive.

★

Chapter 13

The sangria was cool, the *Señora* was gracious, and
Jessie wondered how to ease the conversation into the
reason she was visiting. Yet one did not rush into serious
negotiations; the Spanish considered it rude to do so. For
some while now they'd all been idly chitchatting, which
was meaningless but got everyone on a relaxed, friendly
footing.

Jessie could hardly *not* be relaxed. She, Ysabelle, and
Ki were on one of the inner patios, seated at a table,
shaded from the warm afternoon sun by a grape-arbored
overhang. It was warm, secluded, and serene within the
home, much more conducive to snoozing than to business. And she could hardly not be friendly. She had the
feeling Ysabelle hadn't played hostess in a long time and
was determined to leave no social stone unturned.

She was still in search of an opening when Ev Moran
entered and did it for her. He was dusty, sweaty, exactly

the way he should look after a day of wrangling stock and crew, and he joined them saying he could only stay a minute, but he had things to discuss with the *Señora* that could wait and wanted to say hello.

Then he asked, "Ki, how's your crystal ball?"

"Pretty foggy at the moment. Why?"

"You're the only one who's ever put a dent in them rustlers. Last night they bushwhacked one of my line riders, shot him dead. Ki, do you have any magical notions about who or where they are?"

Ki grinned. "Jessie?"

"Yes, a fairly good notion," Jessie replied, jumping in. "And in fact, I'm morally certain about the man who bosses them."

"One of those oil workers, I bet," Ysabelle said.

Jessie shook her head. "Opportunity and motive. Oil workers don't have the money or time and aren't in a position to run an outlaw gang. One man who does have opportunity, however, also has the biggest motive—the largest profit from it. Broderick Teague."

Moran balked. "I ain't for liking oil men, but Teague's respectable as an old maid. Nobody's seen him do wrong."

"And you said the boss wasn't an oil man," Ysabelle mocked.

"Well, not in the same sense as those oil workers. Teague's an expert geologist, prospector, developer, one of the best. He's certainly expert enough to realize the major oil field is beneath your land with its greatest deposit not far from this house."

Moran gaped. Ysabelle, bewildered but not one at a loss for words, asked, "You truly believe that?"

Concisely, Jessie related how, while riding with Ferguson, she deduced this whole area had once been a sea, its bed sloping north to south. "The flow's toward here;

the sea stayed here, so more oil formed here. Of course, later upheavals altered the surface, until now the desert looks to be the low point of a wedge. But none of that shifted the original slope, or oil pool, far underneath."

Ysabelle was skeptical. "You deduce—how do you know?"

"You showed me. Remember, at that creek, when you said the oil sprayed from the wells and seeped up from pressure under the desert? The spray, I doubt. The seepage is true, but there's too much around for it just to be oozing all this distance. And if such pressure was so strong, then the oil'd be more apt to pop up in the desert, which it doesn't. Actually, the field lacks gas pressure, a common sign of a minor strike, a bywash, and rarely of a main one."

Moran gave a snort. "T'hell where it's from; it's coming out here and poisoning our stock. We need less dribblin', not more."

"Nonsense. Oil doesn't kill cows. Gas will, natural gas that forces oil up as it escapes from faults and fissures. A breeze will dissipate it, but on a still day or at night, gas'll pocket down and be deadly. Your cows were asphyxiated." Jessie turned to Ysabelle. "That's why the buzzards wouldn't peck at any carcass. They know which way the wind *isn't* blowing."

"Cursed by oil, now by gas," Ysabelle said, sighing. "I hope there isn't much more about our range. It's dangerous! If Teague is guilty of nothing else, he somehow unleashed a plague on us."

"Well, gas goes with oil. The oil here hasn't been sprouting much, so probably the gas isn't either. The simple explanation for your plague, I think, is that when Teague brought in his wells, the disturbance underground cracked the cap rock, allowing some leaks."

"Simple when you know all about it. Have you studied it?"

"A few courses," Jessie admitted. "Most of what I've learned I picked up traveling with my late father to projects and such."

"Still," Ysabelle continued, "it's hardly fair to accuse Teague because he may also know of oil under my land. He sent a man once to try and buy an acreage, open and honorably, you know."

"I'm not surprised, and no, there's nothing wrong in that."

"There is more," Ki stated and revealed how he'd spotted Teague's man Whitey with the rustlers, and how Billy the Buck had ambushed them and how his horse had wandered back to Teague's stable. That perked up their ears, and he added, "Recall the pocket caked with oily grit? And we figured the rustler could've labored at the oil field for cover? Well, who'd have hired him? Whitey. First time Jessie, I, and Alice visited Teague, Whitey thought we were there for employment, and as much said he was the recruiter."

"I do begin to see a tie-in," Ysabelle declared.

Ki nodded, but it was Jessie who went on. "Teague really gave himself away when he left himself as virtually the only suspect."

"How's that?"

"The firing of the oil well. For a crew of cowhands to've known how to fire a well is unbelievable, and for a Cartinas hand to've gotten access to it is even more so. An oil worker has knowledge and access, but he'd know what such a fire could do, flash-spread and raze an entire field. He'd be a maniac to risk his life and livelihood."

"Truer still for the well's owner, no?" Ysabelle asked.

163

"No. Teague isn't a worker and didn't need to stick around afterwards—sneak in, sneak out fast. If seen, so what, he'd have acted normal. Second, he hasn't an alibi. He told me earlier at his house he was riding to the field, but he never showed, as Ki will vouch. Third, if the fire had helped him gain his ends, the well or even the field would have been a small loss. He knows all he's drilled into there is a mere eddy of the real pool here. No, the fire was purely a tactic, one of many, in his scheme to wrest control of your land."

Ysabelle frowned quizzically. "How would that help?"

"The same way our feuding helps. Teague figures if he can stoke up enough real hot trouble between you and everyone else, cowmen and oil men alike, you will inevitably get burned and go down. The Cartinas legends and aversion to neighbors were smoke screens in this. When the gas and oil began ruining things here, it only made you pricklier, and it played into Teague's hands. He had our stock stolen and poisoned, then, to fan the flames still more."

"Well, for a tactic, rustlin' beats all others," Moran declared. "We can't sell missing cows, and I hafta 'fess, if we'd lost our big herd yesterday, we'd have been bleeding bad."

"You'd be bled until the only remaining cash asset was the land," Jessie said. "Then he'd come and offer to buy again."

"Thieving hound!" Ysabelle exclaimed. "If he is so *malo*, why not arrest him, have your gringo law stretch his neck?"

"We haven't a shred of proof that'd stand in court," Ki answered and shook his head. "If we'd caught some rustlers at the gorge yesterday, chances are they'd have talked to save their necks, but they all got away. We have to nab them and Teague red-handed."

"But who knows when or where they'll strike next?"

"We will, Ysabelle, if we bait a trap to lure them into it. That's why I'm here; that's what I want you to help us to do."

"To help? To join with you and your ranch?"

Jessie nodded emphatically. There was an uncomfortably long silence, Ysabelle and Moran both staring dubiously. Finally Moran, with a grumbling cough, crossed his arms and scowled at Ki.

"This is when you ask me to honor my debt, I suppose," he growled. "I owe it, Ki, but to you, not to a bunch of others."

"I won't press it," Ki replied. "I will say working with folks usually turns out better than always bucking them. And you're liable to learn they aren't much different from yourself."

Moran muttered, but apparently couldn't think of an argument to put up. He eyed Ysabelle. "I dunno. Something's gotta be done."

"True..." She smiled. "My eyes have been widened these last days. I'll take a chance and try helping you trap the rustlers. What does my good neighbor want us to do?"

"I want you to sink an oil well."

That produced another pair of stares.

"I want the news spread around Vinada that you believe oil is here," Jessie pursued. "See Teague; ask his advice. Tell your banker you're investing the herd money and're wondering about loans. Have your men, the ones who can hold their liquor, boast in the saloons of the anticipated strike and how they'll all become rich."

"Si, but will there truly be this well?"

"There has to be bait showing, Ysabelle, when they're

lured to the trap. A dummy derrick and platform, it won't take much."

Moran said, "I'm addled, Why's it a trap?"

"I'm playing a hunch," Jessie explained, "that the last thing Teague wants to happen is for you to discover the real value of the land. He'll have to stop the drilling. It isn't hard to blow in a bore, if you know how, but it's not a chore to trust to a hired gun. He'll do the job himself. Then, snap! I figure it's worth a try, anyway. Let Teague keep running around loose, and there's bound to be more trouble flaring, more good men dying."

Ysabelle's face grew somber as she glanced toward the room where her husband remained unmoving. "We'll do it," she said.

Jessie and Ki spent the rest of the day and much of the next touring for a suitable location to set the trap.

In the neighborhood of the oil-streaked creek they'd first seen, they found a hollow that was tucked in the crescent of a low ridge and was almost spongy with the seepage staining the grass. The ridge reared a score or more yards south of the hollow, while to the west and east the growth was thin for a long way. From the north was the only practicable route for stealthy approach. They were satisfied. The hollow was a good compromise between a logical well site and the need for high-ground concealment.

Promptly began the work of erecting the fake rig. Soon Vinada was buzzing with the news of Cartinas's sinking a well there in that hollow. Moran reported that Teague advised to stop wasting money and energy, denouncing the project as folly. Teague continued to belittle it in public, citing geological chapter and verse why oil only existed under the desert, his gospel carrying authority and being accepted on faith. Swiftly the general concensus of opinion became that the Cartinas mob had finally gone mad.

Meanwhile, chosen hands from both ranches completed the well and put it into operation, All day a little steam boiler snorted and belched, and a derrick jigged on a shortened rope, with a phony steel bit clanking against a phonier casing. The noise traveled afar; the drilling site appeared robustly active.

There wasn't need for the hands to play oil workers, save for two to watch things and feed the boiler. Yet during its short existence, the well became a gathering point for men from either ranch who chanced to be close or had the hankering. Rivalry persisted, but of a good-natured sort; it was downright impossible, under the circumstances, to remain feuding for long.

Whenever in town, the Cartinas hands would pass along the latest progress at the well. The fastest method of spreading word, however, was for Ysabelle to tell her cook, who told her relatives, who told the world. Heavy fumes were increasingly rising from the bore . . . A layer of rock was struck . . . The drill was through the rock and into a belt of sand . . . Now another layer of rock had been hit, undoubtedly the cap rock, but getting through it to the oil is slow . . .

And every night, a quarter of the crew from each ranch, along with Jessie and Ki, would perch in the brush and rocks and contours of the ridge. On alternate nights, either Ferguson or Moran was there, too, helping guard the rig that loomed dark and silent in the hollow.

Ferguson grew doubtful. "Jessie, I've a notion Teague has pulled in his horns. Everything's been mighty quiet all over of late. Nothing's happened to us or Cartinas since we started pulling together this dog-and-pony show."

"Naturally," she replied, smiling back at him in the

dimness. "It convinces me Teague's hearing and believing our guff, and's figuring our stage-set to be of utmost importance. So he's being smart not to stir up the area now or take chances with anything."

"If it's so important, why hasn't he attacked?"

"Don't forget, he'll want Cartinas to spend as much money as possible before making his move. It'll come very soon, I guarantee. Moran sent a couple of hands to get supplies and to brag about how tomorrow a dynamite charge will be dropped to blow the cap rock. That'd be liable to bring in the well, and Teague knows it. So that's apt to bring Teague to stop the strike before it starts."

Night stretched on, with an overcast sky through which filtered a vague sheen of moonlight. Objects down in the hollow were shadowy, almost ghostly, the well platform nebulous and the tower a phantom tracery in the low murky darkness . . . Jessie and the men remained concealed across the curving slope of the ridge, moving little, eating cold food and lighting smokes carefully, trying to stay comfortable while keeping watchful and alert.

Midnight came and went. The quiet continued undisturbed.

And then, a faint pattering abruptly broke the silence. The sound drew steadily nearer, gradually loudening to a slow beat of horses' irons crossing rocky soil.

"So Teague's gobbled the bait, like you predicted."

Jessie nodded. "But he's not sprung the trap yet, Ian."

"I'll see to it nothing prevents him." Ferguson eased away and began gliding stealthily from one positioned man to another, murmuring encouragements. "Don't get antsy, boys; you know what to wait for. Then show 'em how sharp we've filed our claws . . ."

Shortly a dark, bobbing cluster came into view. The mass rode in quietly from the north, as anticipated, and halted cautiously just inside the opening of the hollow. There was the creak of saddle leather as the raiders dismounted. The hands up along the crescent ridge settled tight with weapons ready, eager yet waiting, having no inclination to fight blindly.

Below in the hollow, Ki crouched unmoving at the fringe of the southern approach. He estimated the force to number upwards of twenty, perhaps more, as they stole forward on foot toward the well. Their features were shrouded by the dark, though he could discern they wore leather and Stetsons and holstered sidearms—they could have almost passed for crew from Jessie's or Cartinas's ranch.

The indistinct forms merged with the deeper shadows of the platform and derrick. There was a mutter of low voices.

Then a tiny spark as Ki struck a match.

Then a baffled howl, "What kinda crazy rig is this?"

Then a blinding flash, gouting yellowish smoke, as a huge pile of oil-soaked waste and brush heaped beside Ki burst into flame. The leaping blaze lit up the hollow and outlined the raiders clustered on and about the platform. For an instant there was the paralysis of utter shock, Ki catching a glimpse of Teague's startled expression and of a figure next to him leaning over the make-believe bore with a blasting cartridge in hand.

Abruptly the man reeled, then pitched off the platform, one boot higher than his head. Jessie's bullet through his chest had been as wholly unexpected as the bonfire. It sent the raiders scrambling, whipping out their revolvers. Their shots laced the night, but they were harried and aiming at the memory of her gunflash.

The whiz of bullets acted strongly on Jessie, making her lips grow more full, her nostrils flare slightly, as she swiftly levered her carbine and triggered again. And the men strung out around her, seething to exact vengeance, fired rounds of stinging, well-directed gunfire. The raiders, silhouetted by roaring flames, dove for their horses or scattered for closer cover, firing as they ran, yelling in agony and dropping in their tracks.

The fast-snapping, brutally shutting guntrap raged as those on the ridge charged impulsively down the slope. Ki, from his vantage, scanned the hollow for Teague, but couldn't spot him among the fleeing or fallen. He sprinted hunched toward the far side, where he had last glimpsed Teague heading, and was almost there when a raider reared in the way, blasting as fast as he could hammer.

But Ki was no longer there. Springing high, Ki lashed out kicking, ramming his foot into the gunman's face, fracturing the skull like an egg and driving shards of broken bone into the brain. The man went down and Ki went on without hardly missing a stride.

Bullets were flailing about like a horde of wasps, and the air fairly sizzled with gunfire. Something slammed into the earth scant inches from Ki, kicking dirt up in his face, and from somewhere on the ridge drifted the crack of a rifle. Ki slewed aside, while staring at the slope with suspicion. A slug sang angrily over his head. A third, now, flicked chips off a boulder a little to his right. A raider, he realized, must have managed to weasel through, climb up behind them, and was firing a rifle.

"Ki!" Jessie cried out. "There's Whitey!"

Ki swerved again. Whitey, snarling, a revolver clenched in his unwounded hand, loomed before him. Both men acted at the same instant, Whitey's heavy Colt .45 erupting pointblank. Ki felt a smarting along his left thigh. But Whitey was toppling backwards, with Ki's *shuriken* imbedded deep into the bridge of his nose.

"Thanks, Jessie," Ki called, then swore as another low-flying slug ripped into the ground between them. "Watch out! One of Teague's men snuck up on the ridge. Have you seen Teague?"

"No, d'you think he got away?"

"He better not have."

"Won't do him much good. We nailed him with his gang."

"I wonder if he's the sniper. If he knows he's got nothing to lose, he might stick to kill us first and then—" Ki suddenly ducked, lead keening past his ear. "Whoever it is, he's getting the range and'll plug us sooner or later. Maybe I can stop him."

Ki darted for the slope. Impatient as he was, he forced himself to climb carefully, to converge silently. The fire in the hollow cast flickering light, but it was still difficult to distinguish between substance and shadow, and he had to rely on the spurts of gunfire to guide him toward the sniper's nook.

Finally he could dimly make out the Stetson and torso of a man on a shallow stone ledge, kneeling on one knee while shouldering a Winchester Express repeater. Ki began a slow stalk, careful in case the sniper should hear something and shoot at the noise. A pebble rolled, clicking against another. The sniper glanced toward it, but Ki was motionless, invisible against the boulders—although he was so near he could hear the man swearing irritably and slapping at biting insects.

The man was not Teague, but the sound of his gutteral cursing did something to Ki's expression, making it thin-lipped and narrow-eyed. For Ki recognized the voice, having heard it before through the door of the second floor room of the Poinsettia Hotel. This was the man Ki suspected to be a top confederate of Teague's, possibly second in line, but certainly high in the chain of command.

Ki was a breathless statue until the man turned away again. Then Ki closed in. Whipping his left hand out, Ki grasped the man's gunwrist in an *atemi* hold that caused him to drop the rifle. At the same time, the rock-hard heel of Ki's right hand shot forward and smashed the man squarely between the eyes. As the unconscious man started to fall, Ki simply embraced him and dragged him away a few feet, then sent him rolling down the grade into a scalloped nest of rocks, like the cranny of a cracked tooth, where Ki figured he would lay peacefully comatose for the next twelve hours at least.

Time enough for Ki to return and ask questions.

Ki hastened down the slope to the hollow. The battle had lost its initial savage punch, but there was still deadly skirmishing going on. The hands, who'd been courageous before when attacked by the raiders, were ferocious now in dishing out retribution. Of the raiders, some had died, some had escaped, a few had surrendered; those remaining were bottled here and there under isolated cover, fighting stubbornly against being dislodged.

High-pocket waved at Ki and shouted proudly, "Plugged three an' bagged three prisoners. I'll win my new saddle yet, by gad!"

"Was any of them Teague?"

"Nope, he wasn't."

Jessie and Ferguson were hurrying across to Ki, and as they came up, Ferguson hooted over at High-pocket, "You'll see the saddle when you buy it for me! Hey!" The *hey* was at the same moment he touched Ki by the sleeve. "Hey, looky at the sky yonder, will you?"

From some distance away and rising above the crest

of the ridge, a reddish glow was visible against the darker hillscape beyond.

"Coming from the direction of the ranch," Ki said.

"It is?" Jessie then gasped with realization. "Cartinas's home is afire! Another group of the gang must've hit there, having been sent, I bet, to wipe it out while the well here was being blown up."

Ferguson grunted. "Teague had an ace up his sleeve, eh."

Jessie nodded bleakly. "I never figured on a two-prong raid."

"Nobody but Teague would've, either." Ki snapped, wheeling. "Quick, let's grab the men and see if we can't trump his trick yet."

"Hold it," Ferguson protested. "We pull out, and the rats we done cornered here will scamper free. Liable to head there, too, and then like as not corner us betwixt them and that second bunch."

"We'll take who we can, and leave enough here to finish things," Jessie argued urgently. "Look at it this way, Ian. Teague isn't here. If I'm not mistaken, he's on a beeline for the ranch to join the only force he's got left. And Teague is the one we're after."

Ferguson blinked, seeing the truth of this. "I'll put High-pocket in charge of mopping up," he said, turning to lope away.

By the time they were in saddle and galloping pell-mell for Cartinas's hacienda, they could see the first distinct tongues of flame eating into the three generations of fine old buildings.

★

Chapter 14

The fire was an intense magnet. It provoked nine of them, including a mix of hands from both ranches, into riding headlong as a hard, compact knot, prodding them to drive straight toward the blaze without attention to trails, terrain, or footing.

As she rode, Jessie also felt drawn by an image of Ysabelle, a picture of her desperation, her anguished certainty that after tonight there would no longer be a Cartinas Grant, a Cartinas domain. And, as well, Jessie felt compelled by her own desire to retaliate against Teague, to square accounts for his treacherous ambition, and to settle the score for his duplicity, his betrayal of her faith in him. That image and that vengeance flagged Jessie on.

They reined in at the grove of oaks near the main house. To their relief they saw that fire had not yet touched it, though some of the smaller buildings by the corral were already tumbling infernos. Ev Moran's boys, out-numbered by Teague's gang, were making a stubborn, withdrawing fight, which had its magnificence but which could in the end only delay the inevitable. A small party of defenders appeared to be in the house, which was now suffering the heaviest attack. Others of the Cartinas crew were positioned below the corral in a log wagon shed that offered some shelter.

Jessie pointed out this shed. "Get down that way as best you can," she instructed Ferguson. "See if you can pry those men free; then the bunch of you start working back up across the yard. Maybe combined we'll be enough to break them before they get the house, too."

Anxiously Ferguson asked, "But what about you?"

Jessie then pointed to scurrying figures shuttling across the yard. "Teague's down there somewhere, and I aim to find him."

Reluctant to leave her and Ki alone, Ferguson never-theless obeyed, and he and the six hands branched off afoot. Also afoot, Jessie and Ki cut straight into the open, running easily and with their eyes on the shifting pack of Teague's gunnies flinging repeated attacks at the house. For long seconds they went unnoticed. A gunman paused to watch them, seemed almost convinced they were two of the raiders, then bellowed sudden alarm. Some of those in front by the veranda lanced a hot fire at them, making them break stride and dive behind the cordwood stacked on the edge of the woodlot.

Another man was behind this shelter. They smelled him before they saw him, for the vague odor of blood hung close to the earth. The man lay face down. Ki rolled him over, his fingers swiftly turning gentle when he re-alized the man was badly wounded. He was still breath-ing, however. The face, turned up, was highlighted by

175

the glow of fire. The man was Ev Moran.

Moran's eyes fluttered open. He stared at Ki, then at Jessie, and a crooked grin etched his pain-grimaced lips. He tried twice before he could form words. "Grand . . . idea o' yours," he wheezed. "They struck . . . us instead."

Jessie, kneeling, smiled tenderly. "They struck us, too."

"Glad to see some o' you made . . ." Moran stopped, choking up.

A heavy crash sounded across the yard, and firing from the house began to ebb. Jessie straightened, thinking Ferguson and the hands must have reached the trapped Cartinas crew below the corral. But Teague's men had a ram against the front door of the house, and Jessie doubted that Ferguson, even if reinforced by those crewmen, could get back up across the yard in time. She glanced back down at Moran. The foreman had slumped, and Ki was drawing the lids of his eyes closed. Ki stood up then, shaking his head.

They didn't speak; there wasn't time, and there wasn't anything to be said that couldn't wait for a eulogy later. Together they raced the length of the woodpile and launched from behind it at full speed. Guns opened up sporadically at them, but there were not as many as they had expected. Either the Cartinas crewmen were keeping a lot of Teague's occupied around the shed, or their own men had cut the odds down considerably in the savage yard fighting. Or both.

Teague and four or five others—Jessie couldn't tell with certainty—were up on the veranda. They vanished, and she realized the door had finally been battered down by their ram. They surged on, the house seeming at an impossible distance. Then at last they felt the veranda steps underfoot and saw the black maw of the shattered

176

doorway dead ahead—dead being the big word.

Heedless, they plowed through it. A gunman was crouched, revolver up, by a lamp across the room. Jessie and Ki parted, each springing to one side, as the revolver bucked and lead speared through the open doorway where they'd been. With the door frame at his back, Ki snapped a dagger across the room and the gunman went over thrashing. A dead man lay across the threshold of a corridor, from which echoed the pounding of heavy boots. They angled toward it, hearing a woman's shrill cry above the bootfalls. They jumped the corpse and started along the corridor, recalling from having been here before that it led to Ramon Cartinas's room.

Not far ahead of them, a man turned around to identify them. Jessie shot him with a quick upward tilt of her custom .38 pistol, which drove a bullet through his brisket and smashed his spine. The man tilted, crumbling. They dodged his fall and moved on fast. Another gunnie ducked out of an adjacent door, almost colliding with Ki, and Jessie cut him down with a hard, merciless swing of the barrel of her gun. She hoped they'd find Teague this way and Ysabelle, too, in time.

A door gaped open at the end of the hall, the door to Ramon Cartinas's room. They sped for it, and when they closed to where they could glimpse through the doorway, they saw a peculiar tableau in the room beyond. Broderick Teague was standing with his back to them, and Ysabelle was caught in the corner he was facing, his position in the room preventing her from dodging out of it. Her face was incredibly ashen for one of her heritage, the pallor accentuated by the rich blackness of her hair. Her eyes were widened in a strange mixture of mortal fear and dazed admiration. And Teague's head was turned so that his gaze was following Ysabelle's.

Jessie understood none of this. Neither did Ki. They understood only that Teague was before them, that Teague had begun this, and that with Teague's end, this treachery would end with him. They understood that if Teague wished to end it by dying, they would gladly honor his last request. They stepped forward and entered the room.

To one side of the doorway was a man on the floor. They froze in stunned disbelief. The man was Ramon Cartinas, dressed in an invalid's gown and a pair of socks, nothing more, his legs trailing out helplessly behind him. His lips were set and bloody, and a terrible fury roiled in his eyes. His body was quivering, and he clutched clumsily in his two knotted hands a heavy old Remington .44-40, smoke wreathing from its muzzle.

It was only then that they spied the stain on Teague's rumpled suit coat under one armpit and realized he had been shot. Simultaneous with this awareness, the man on the floor fired again. Broderick Teague swiveled slowly, took a long step, and pitched forward onto his face. Ysabelle stumbled from her corner and fell to her knees beside her husband.

"Ramon, Ramon," she sobbed.

He tried to lift his head a little farther. He tried to smile. The thick weapon sagged out of his fingers, his jaw hinging spasmodically, his mouth uttering no sound. And while these things were happening, a tight, white stiffness ran from his face. His entire body eased as if drained, and he slumped, wilting, to lie on the floor with his eyes half-closed. He was dead.

Stricken, Ysabelle looked up mournfully at Jessie and Ki. "He, he dragged himself from his couch to, to protect me. He . . ." She broke off again, weeping, chanting her husband's name.

Ki leaned against the wall and eyed Jessie glumly. "I

think Ramon also knew who'd shot him. Or figured who had it done."

Jessie nodded. "He had more of a grudge to settle than I did."

They heard bootfalls in the corridor and tensed ready, fearing it heralded more Teague gunmen. The footsteps approached at an oddly dragging gait, however, and then came Ferguson's bull-roar voice as he peered in to regard the tragic, bizarre scene.

"Well, if this don't peel the shingles off the barn!"

Ferguson entered favoring his right leg, which was bound at the calf with a grubby, blood-stained bandanna. With him were three crewmen, one Cartinas and two of his own. It was on the Cartinas man that he leaned, though the support that seemed to draw him erect was the concerned look on Ysabelle's face as she rose to her feet.

Chagrined, he said, "Just m' luck. Got it on a first volley." Gruffer then, as if recalling past wrangles with her, he added, "But you got your ranch, *Señora*, with only a few sheds burned."

"You fool," she cried and scanned the crew as she swung toward Jessie and Ki. "You stubborn, fighting, selfless fools!"

Ki grinned. "I think we were fighting for the same thing."

"Cartinas." The word came uncertainly to her.

"Oh, hell, yes," Ferguson replied acidly. "For Cartinas. A Ferguson always gets hisself shot to rags for someone else's ranch."

Ysabelle sucked in her breath. "For the Cartinases, then—the only one who's left. And for my neighbors. For riding with our ranges open and our lines unguarded and our carbines hanging on the bunkhouse walls. There must be happiness in all of this!"

"A couple, countin' the well we hoisted. Make it a real one," Ferguson suggested, brightening. "I mean, if Teague wanted your land so badly, there has to be oil around there. Maybe a fortune."

"Speaking of the well," Ki murmured to Jessie, and explained how, why, and who he'd knocked out up on the ridge.

Jessie frowned thoughtfully, then turned to Ferguson. "Has everything gone all right? Besides your leg, that is."

"Right as rain," he declared. "We whumped 'em down, the whole lot of 'em. Moran got it out behind the woodpile, and three others is tore some, but we didn't get hit bad for what we done."

"Then I believe Ki and I will be going," Jessie said. "It's important we clear up any loose ends as quickly as possible."

Ferguson and Ysabelle gave them questioning glances, but Jessie and Ki were already moving from the room. As they headed along the hall, they heard Ferguson returning to his suggestion, "P'raps a fortune, I tell you, and if you needed some help—"

"Fortune!" Ysabelle scoffed. "How can money replace the land the oil ruins, land that was bought with the blood of Spanish kings?"

"The devil! Still snobbin' up your blasted ranch!"

Then they heard one of the crewmen bark disgustedly, "Tarnation! Stop arguing and let's get you flattened and patched!"

And smiling amusedly at each other, Ki and Jessie passed through the smashed front doorway and walked to their horses in the grove.

The moon was low and stars powdered the sky as they

set out on their return to the fake drilling rig. Darkness still clung to the cracks and crevices, but it was by the gray light of a new dawn that they entered the hollow. The fighting had long ceased, High-pocket and the others who'd remained were cleaning up, trussing the last of the prisoners. Wrists tied to saddle horns, roped in bunches, the sullen-eyed desperados had come to the end of their tethers.

They paused there, and High-pocket came over to exchange doings. He mopped the dust and sweat from his weathered face and grinned up.

"How'd it go?" he asked.

"About the same as here from what I can see," Jessie replied.

"Thems you don't see, we've already buried," High-pocket declared proudly. "We lost our share too, but we're wagoning them home with the wounded. Anyhow, the rustlers are through, Teague is through, and by gadfry, I'm nie to tuckered through myself. S'long."

Smiling, they snapped quick, informal gestures of salute and rode across to the base of the ridge. They dismounted, tethered their horses, and started climbing the slope on foot.

"I hope you put this fellow sound asleep and tucked him in good," Jessie said, as Ki sought the hole in which he'd rolled the sniper. "If he's important as you figure he is, then with Teague gone, he's about the only one left who can supply the details of the operation."

"Will you stop stewing? He'll still be there."

The man was, lying stiff and motionless at the bottom of the narrow depression below the ledge. Since it lacked space for all three of them, Ki stood on the edge while Jessie slid down to the man.

"Ki, he's as dead as a doornail!" she exclaimed.

Bracing a foot behind her on the cracked, crumbled rock, she grabbed the man to turn him onto his back. From the force of her shifting leverage, her foot broke through the rubbled surface, and she sank almost to her knee, swearing most unladylike as she struggled to recover her balance. Then she wrestled the man over and knelt. The man's face was swollen and mottled a ghastly purple.

"You must've hit him too hard, Ki, crushed his windpipe or something. He looks like he choked or suffocated. By heaven, he also looks familiar. Where . . ." Jessie stopped talking, weariness passing over her features. She brushed imaginary cobwebs from her eyes. "Rudolph Aubrecht, now I remember. The cartel liaison and troubleshooter we almost nabbed in St. Louis." Her speech was thickening, alarming Ki. "Beginning to make sense . . . how Teague . . . financed . . . managed all his shenanigans . . ." She stretched a hand to steady herself, then silently keeled over atop Aubrecht's body.

"Jessie!" Bending low and reaching, Ki seized a limp arm and dragged Jessie from the cranny. He glimpsed the crevice her boot had gone through, but paid it no mind as he hastily laid Jessie out and started fanning her face with his hat. "C'mon, snap out of it!"

Jessie was breathing in gasps that seemed tortured. Her face had become sickly, bluish under her creamy bronze suntan. As Ki worked over her, however, her breathing returned to normal and after a few minutes she opened her eyes, weakly licking at her lips.

"What . . . hit me?"

"You fainted, Jessie."

"Fainted? Me? I never faint, Ki, as you better well know." She sat up, then stood thoughtfully, and then as though to prove her momentary weakness was not her

182

fault, she said, "Give me a match."

Ki handed her his container of matches. She struck one and tossed it into the cranny. Before it landed, there was a startling whoosh, and a sheet of intensely hot, bluish flame spurted upward.

Ki backed hastily. "Gas! A pocket of natural gas."

"With good pressure behind it. The surface must be more fragmented and fissured than I thought, only the cap rock holding the gas in until Teague fractured it while drilling. No wonder there isn't any pressure at the desert; the gas is all blowing out over here."

"No wonder you got dizzy, after your foot sunk through the crust and enlarged that hole. And that's what killed Aubrecht, not me. He was lying over the leak long enough for the gas to finish him."

"C'mon, let's throw some rocks and dirt over the fire before it gets cooking."

They worked frantically and cut off the crevice so that the blue flame dwindled and snuffed out. Ki, his eyebrows and lashes singed, stared at the smoldering cranny and blackened vegetation.

"Two vast fortunes for the price of one grab."

"Exactly, Ki. Teague would've known the gas here is extensive, probably have even estimated how much. He'd have known gas makes better light than oil, and is easier to handle, and that he could pipe it to Vinada or wherever for less cost. It doubled his greed."

"I'm curious about what triggered it in the first place. He wasn't bad when your father knew him, y'know, and I'd liked to've asked Teague why and when it was that something bent wrong in him."

Jessie shrugged and began strolling slowly, aimlessly up the ledge. "Maybe years ago. Or maybe now, when all this came up. Maybe he honestly miscalculated about the desert and speculated so heavily that when he saw his error, he realized he was ruined. Or maybe it was his pride, the ego of an expert with egg on his face."

Ki fell in alongside her. "Well, for whatever reason, Teague became like all crooks. He couldn't be satisfied with his deal with you, or with convincing the Cartinases to go shares with him for a decent split. He had to try and take over everything."

"And taking over takes money and experience. It kept pestering me where and how Teague got them. My first inkling came with Billy the Buck, but I wasn't sure until I saw *him*—" She thumbed toward the hole. "Enter Rudy Aubrecht, providing the cash, gunmen, and expertise, acting as Teague's segundo while watching over the cartel's investment. The cartel would've been induced in by the opportunity to corner this region's oil and gas development, but I think the kicker was that they'd be sticking it to me while they were at it."

"That explains Aubrecht sniping at us, I imagine. Teague was washed up by then, but if Aubrecht could down us, he'd earn a bonus from the cartel and have a fair chance at reorganizing the gang, jumping the Cartinases again, and winding up with the goodies."

They reached the ledge. A faintly soughing breeze caressed them and then flirted away. Cream streaked with rose banded the eastern horizon, forecasting the approach of another sunny day. Jessie and Ki stood there, quietly contemplative, gazing out over the hollow and surveying the placid expanse of range and hill.

Until Jessie remarked, "It'll change, Ki. It'll become tall derricks and noisy pumps and skeins of piping and valves. And Ysabelle will be right; the land will be scarred and spoiled."

"You're sure she'll allow that? She's sure she won't."

"She'll change, too. She already has. She's learned what can happen when neighbors get on the prod for one another and make it easy for smart outlaws to slide in and cause havoc. And call it a baseless hunch of mine, but I suspect Ian will enact an earnest good neighbor policy, once the widow's grieving period is over."

Ki grinned wryly. "Well, the way they were squabbling when we left, you'd think they were an old married couple. But Ysabelle is a wildcat, Jessie, and wildcats stay independent and wild."

"Ysabelle will never be a mild-mannered little pet tabby," Jessie allowed with a laugh. "But she knows, even if she's not yet admitted it to herself, that she's paid her debt to the Cartinas clan. She's started thinking of herself, for herself, and to change."

This, then, which should have been an end, was merely a beginning. The Cartinas legend would flourish, despite the death of Ramon, the last pure blood of the line. His terrific will that had driven the crippled old man to save his wife and slay Broderick Teague was the stuff of which legends are born. And whether it be Ferguson or another lucky suitor, eventually a man would win Ysabelle and sire new generations in that comfortable old home and keep alive the traditions of wild males and beautiful females. And there would be no Teague or cartel to warp the truth.

This, Jessie thought serenely, made it all worthwhile.

Look for

LONE STAR AND THE ALASKAN GUNS

fortieth novel in the exciting
LONE STAR
series from Jove

coming in December!